CON

INTRODUCTION

Here's a quick question for you. Is your geography teacher an alien from outer space? (Warning: Think very carefully before you answer unless you *want* to do extra geography homework for the rest of your schooldays.)

On second thoughts, you might be better off keeping your ideas to yourself. Mind you, it can be horribly tricky telling the difference between your teacher and an alien. Your teacher might as well be from outer space for all the sense she makes. Can you understand a word she's saying?

A normal person would simply say, "In the rainforest you can't see the wood for the trees." See what I mean? Obviously your teacher is "barking" mad. But don't be too tough on your crackpot teacher. Horrible geography can be baffling enough for human beings, let alone for aliens with two heads *and* two brains. But just imagine if your teacher really did come from another planet. What on Earth would she make of your weird world? Picture the scene. You're sitting in on double geography on far-off Planet Blob...

TODAY'S LESSON IS ALL ABOUT THE PLANET CALLED "EARTH". OBSERVE THE STRANGE, ALIEN LANDSCAPE. EARTHLINGS CALL THE GREEN BLOBS YOU CAN SEE ON THE MAP "RAINFORESTS". TO FIND OUT MORE ABOUT THEM, OPEN YOUR EARTH FILE DATA BANK FOR THE LATEST INTERPLANETARY REPORT...

WHO?

Interplanetary report number BLOB delta 5.1
Star date: 170361

Mission: To observe Planet Earth. (Earthlings call this activity "geography".)

Destination: The bloomin' rainforest

Background: Tests reveal that rainforests are hot, wet and humid (that's Earth-speak for stickily warm). They're packed with tall, woody life-forms called "trees". The forests cover just 6 per cent of the land on Earth but they are inhabited by half of all Earth plants and animals. Watch this space. Further observations will be made.

Report conclusion: In their Earth schools, juvenile Earthlings are informed about rainforests by adult Earthlings called "geography teachers". Meanwhile, Earthlings are chopping the rainforests down for farms and roads.

WARNING! *This is not logical.*

(Obviously geography lessons are just as boring on Planet Blob as they are on Planet Earth!)

Still, rainforests are what this book is all about. Wet enough to soak you to the skin, hot and sticky even in the middle of winter, and home to more creepy-crawlies than ANYWHERE ELSE ON EARTH, rainforests will soon start to grow on you. In *Bloomin' Rainforests*, you can…

- have dinner with the dinosaurs who lived in the first ever rainforests.
- find out why some weird forest fungi glow in the dark.

- learn how to hunt wild animals with the local rainforest people.
- sniff out flowers that stink of smelly socks with top botanist*, Fern. Phwoar!

(*That's the posh name for a horrible scientist who studies plants.)

This is geography like never before. And it's tree-mendously exciting. But if you're thinking of "branching" out on your own, keep your wits about you. Rainforests aren't all about pretty flowers and tropical fruit trees. They can be horribly wild and dangerous. You'll need eyes in the back of your head as you watch out for jaguars on the look-out for lunch, butterflies as big as birds, spiders the size of school dinner-plates and bizarre meat-eating plants.

Whatever you do, stick close to the path – it's easy to get lost. Dead easy. And it can happen to anyone. Even the experts sometimes get it horribly wrong. Which is exactly what happened to intrepid explorer, Percy Fawcett. One fine day, he set off to explore the South American rainforest … and was never seen again. You can read his terrible true story overleaf.

LOST IN THE JUNGLE

London, England, 1906

The dashing young officer with the bushy moustache knocked smartly on the old oak door.

"Come in," boomed a clipped, gruff voice. The officer opened the door and peeked inside the gloomy room. Behind a large desk piled high with dusty maps and books, sat a stern-looking man.

"Ah, Fawcett, good to see you, old chap," he said. "I've got a little job for you. Ever been to Bolivia, dear boy?"

The man was the President of the Royal Geographical Society of Great Britain, an association which mapped and sent explorers to every corner of the globe. His visitor that day was army colonel and all-round good egg, Percy H Fawcett. The President lost no time in explaining what he wanted Fawcett to do. It went something like this...

The Bolivian government wanted some brand-new maps made of their country and they'd asked the Royal Geographical Society for help. And this was where good old Percy came in. Apart from being brave, strong and as tough as old boots, Percy was also a crack cartographer (that's the posh name for a horrible geographer who draws up maps). Just the man for the Bolivian job.

There was just one teeny problem. To make his maps at all accurate, he was going to have to travel through some horribly perilous places. Places where no outsiders had ever been before. Places where the locals didn't take kindly to strangers. Even if Percy survived all that, he might be struck down by a deadly disease or eaten alive by a peckish jaguar. Either way, he'd be a goner. This was no job for a feeble or faint-hearted person!

But plucky Percy wasn't feeble or faint-hearted. Far from it. And he didn't need to be asked twice. In fact, he jumped at the chance to have the adventure of a lifetime. Born by the seaside in Devon, England, in 1867, adventure was Percy's middle name. (His real middle name was Harrison but you get the point.) From an early age, Percy wanted to see the world. Sadly, until he was nineteen years old, all he saw was dull old Devon. Then he joined the British army and was sent off to Sri Lanka, Ireland and Malta. But Percy soon got fed up with army life. It was just too bloomin' boring. Real-life adventure was what he was after. And that's exactly what he got.

South America, 1906-1914

In June 1906, Percy arrived in La Paz, Bolivia, ready to embark on his great adventure. First stop was lofty Lake Titicaca, high up in the peaky Andes Mountains. Getting to the lake was a very rocky road. The thin mountain air made breathing difficult and the mules kept losing their footing on the steep mountain slopes. But did Percy lose heart? Nope, he didn't. Our gutsy hero simply gritted his teeth and plodded grimly on. It would take more than a slippery slope to trip him up. Next, he charted the sources of several raging rivers that poured into the awesome Amazon, and still had time to explore the mighty Mato Grosso (part of the Amazon rainforest in neighbouring Brazil).

If hiking up mountains wasn't tough enough, hacking through the Mato Grosso rainforest really tested his mettle. The flies, the heat, the constant damp really took their toll on Percy and his companions. Before very long, their clothes were soaked through. Then they began to turn mouldy. Day after day, the men chopped their way through a green tangle of vines as thick as human legs and strangling, snake-like creepers. Around every corner danger lurked.

Take gigantic snakes, for starters. One day, Percy and his local guides were paddling gently down river. Imagine the scene. It was a warm, sunny day and life was grand. Percy may well have been whistling. But the peace and quiet didn't last long. Suddenly their flimsy canoe was almost flipped over by … a truly enormous snake. Its great, ugly head reared out of the water, along with several metres of massive coils.

Unluckily for Percy, he was being attacked by a giant anaconda. The biggest snake in the world. Anacondas can grow up to 10 metres long and measure a metre around the middle. They can catch prey as big as deer and goats, and have terrible table manners. First they grab their victims in their colossal coils and squeeze them to death.

Then they swallow their supper whole. Nasty, very nasty. Was our Percy petrified? Was he, heck. Quick as a flash, he grabbed his gun and shot the revolting reptile stone dead.

And that wasn't all. Another time, Percy and his party were fired on by unfriendly locals. (They only stopped when Percy got out his accordion and started to sing. It must have scared them to death!)

They were harassed by hideous, hairy spiders, bitten half to death by vicious vampire bats and charged at by a bunch of wild bulls. One man even had his fingers chomped off by piranha fish as he was washing his hands in the river! But wild animals weren't their only worry. Their canoe capsized again in the raging rapids and they were nearly washed away by a waterfall.

And later, they almost starved to death when they ran out of food. For ten long days, they lived on nothing but rancid honey and the odd bird's egg until, more bloomin' dead than alive, they managed to kill a deer. The ravenous men ate every bit of it, right down to its fur. (Bet that got stuck in their teeth.)

Finally, in 1914, his map-making done, Percy returned to England. But there was no time for our horrible hero to rest. He was soon off fighting in World War One. When the war ended, Percy was awarded a top medal for bravery but his army days were over. Despite his brush with starvation and the weird wildlife, he was itching to get back to the rainforest again.

The Amazon rainforest, Brazil, 1925

At last, in spring 1925, Percy set off for Brazil again. He'd been back to the jungle several times in between to get to know the region better. But this time muddlesome maps were the last thing on his mind. You see, for years, Percy had dreamed of a fabulous city with beautiful buildings made from silver and gold, and gorgeous statues made from glittering crystal. He'd read about the city, which he curiously called "Z", in an ancient library book. Now he wanted to see it with his own eyes.

The only snag was that the city was thought to lie right in the middle of the deepest, darkest jungle. Where no outsider had ever set foot before. Did Percy find his long-lost city? Or did he perish in the attempt? Here's how the newspapers of the time might have reported what happened next...

INTREPID EXPLORER STILL MISSING

Concern is growing for plucky British explorer, Colonel Percy H Fawcett, feared lost in the jungle. Fawcett, 58, was last seen in person in April when he and his eldest son, John, set off into the jungle with a family friend, Raleigh Rimell. Their goal was to find a fabulous, long-lost city of gold which Fawcett believed lay in the heart of the rainforest.

FAWCETT & SON

In May, the men said goodbye to their local guides and their faithful packhorses. The tangled terrain made riding difficult so they chose to carry on on foot, alone, carrying their own baggage.

BACK-PACKING

The guides brought back a note from Fawcett for his wife, addressed eerily "Dead Horse Camp". It read, "You need have no fear of any failure." Nothing has been heard from him since.

Despite Fawcett's instructions to his friends that they should not risk their lives trying to rescue him, there are plans to send out a search team soon.

ON THE LOOK OUT

when it comes to exploring. In fact, he's as hard as nails. Besides, he's brilliant at reading maps and he's never, ever got lost before. If anyone can make it out alive, it's our Percy." We hope he is right.

One close friend told our reporter, "Percy's a real pro

Sadly, this was to be Percy's last jungle journey. Search party after search party set out for the forest but no trace of Percy was ever found. Not long afterwards the rumours began. It was difficult to know what to believe. Had Percy been eaten by alligators? Or had he caught a fatal fever and died? Was he hopelessly lost?

HOLD ON! I THINK WE TURN LEFT HERE

Or had he in fact found his city and was he now living there happily ever after? Truth is, nobody knew.

Some years later, one man claimed to have got to the bottom of the mystery, once and for all. He said Percy had been killed by hostile locals and, what's more, he'd got Percy's bones to prove it. Could he be telling the tragic truth? Well, the funny bones were taken off to England and examined by bone experts. But guess what? They turned out to belong to somebody else, after all. So what actually happened to poor lost Percy Fawcett? To this day, nobody really knows.

So, as you can see, rainforests can be horribly dangerous but they're also bloomin' brilliant and fascinating as well. So what on Earth are these perilous places and where can you find one, if you dare? Is it *really* like a jungle out there? Or is their "bark" worse than their bite? You'll find the answers to all of these questions as you "leaf" through this book…

HOT AND STICKY

The best way to find out what a rainforest is like is to go and see one for yourself. But if there isn't a rainforest near where you live, what on Earth can you do? Well, why not try this simple experiment? (Unless you *want* to go without pocket money for the rest of your life, ask permission first.)

Go into your bedroom and turn the heating on full.

Then scatter piles of dead leaves, twigs and mouldy mushrooms all over the floor.

Grab some pot plants (rubber plants work well) and stand them on the ground. (You'll need to pick some good, tall ones for the towering rainforest trees.)

If you're feeling really brave, release a handful of spiders and some creepy-crawlies into the room. They'll give the place a nice, lived-in look.

Now get a watering can and give the whole thing a good soaking. This will make your room horribly hot and steamy. Just like a real rain-forest.

(OK, so it might be better to use your imagination for this last bit.)

First rainforests

The first rainforests grew about 150 million years ago. (Even your teacher isn't that bloomin' old.) These ancient forests were packed with giant conifer trees that dinosaurs once munched. Incredibly, some of these prehistoric plants still grow today. Take maddening monkey-puzzle trees, for example. (You might have seen them growing in gardens.) They got their name because muddled monkeys couldn't puzzle out how to climb up their spiky branches.

There were even bloomin' rainforests in Britain. Don't believe me? Well, it's true. British botanists have found fossil pollen grains from ancient rainforest trees that bloomed about 50 million years ago. (The weather was much warmer then.)

Earth-shattering fact
The name rainforest was coined in the nineteenth century by German geographer and botanist, Alfred Schimper. He thought it fitted because the forests were so bloomin' wet. (OK, so you didn't need to be a brain surgeon to work that out.) Some people call them jungles instead. "Jungle" actually comes from an old Indian word which actually means, er, desert or wasteland! Confusing, or what? Later the word changed to mean a thick tangle of tropical plants and trees. In other words, a bloomin' rainforest.

Where on Earth do bloomin' rainforests grow?

Hi, Fern here. Being a botanist, I'm mad about plants so rainforests are right up my street. So where can you find one if you need one? Well, rainforests cover about six per cent of the Earth – that's about the size of the USA. They grow in three enormous chunks in South America, Africa and South-East Asia with bits and pieces on the Pacific Islands. Down under, Australians also claim to have some in Queensland. So you've probably got quite a long way to go. Here's a handy map to show you where on Earth you can root a rainforest out.

NORTH AMERICA

ATLANTIC OCEAN

ASIA

PAPUA NEW GUINEA

INDIA

AFRICA

VENEZUELA

COLUMBIA

BURMA

PACIFIC OCEAN

ZAIRE

INDIAN OCEAN

BRAZIL

PERU

SOUTH AMERICA

INDONESIA

BOLIVIA

AUSTRALIA

ANTARCTICA

Could you recognize a rainforest?

If you ask a geographer to describe a rainforest, don't worry if he or she starts spouting ancient history…

> *Never have I beheld so fair a thing; trees beautiful and green, with flowers and fruits each according to their kind; many birds, and little birds which sing very sweetly.*

Yuck! Slushy, or what? Actually it was ace explorer, Christopher Columbus, who wrote this in 1492 in a letter to the King and Queen of Spain. But it's no good going all gooey-eyed. In nature, things aren't always quite as pretty and sweet as they first seem. If you want to be a budding geographer, you'll have to do better than that. Wouldn't know a rainforest if it grew in your own back garden? Don't worry. Help is at hand. But first, here's Fern with the rainforest weather forecast…

> Today will start off hot and sticky with clear skies in the morning. It'll cloud over in the afternoon and there's a good chance of a thunderstorm with torrential rain. Don't bother with a brolly — you'll still get soaking wet. Tomorrow will be much the same, and the next day, and the next day, and the day after that…

Anyway, there are three easy ways of recognizing a rainforest by its weird weather. Generally speaking, rainforests are:

Steaming hot
It's always hot in the rainforest, whatever time of the year you go. So if you're hoping for a white Christmas, you're in for a very long wait. In the bloomin' rainforest, it's summer all year long. Temperatures can reach a baking 30°C by day and it's not much cooler at night. And every day's the same. So why are rainforests so horribly hot? Well, it's to do with where on Earth they grow. Rainforests bloom in the steamy tropics along the Equator. (That's an imaginary line around the Earth. It splits the Earth into north and south.) Here the sun always shines straight overhead so its warming rays are seriously strong.

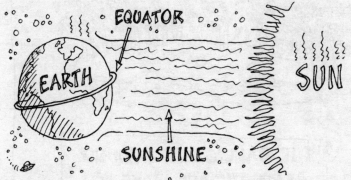

Soaking wet
If you're heading for the rainforest, expect to get wet through. It pours with rain almost every day. Horrible geographers count rainforests as places which get at least 2,000 millimetres of rain a year. Wet, or what? The reason rainforests are so bloomin' wet is because they're so close to the Equator. Here's what happens:

What's more, because it's so wet and hot, the rain that falls on the forest trees quickly evaporates (turns into water gas). Then the warm air rises and forms clouds, then it pours with rain all over again. And it never rains but it pours. Sometimes 60 millimetres of rain can fall in one single hour. Which might not sound much, but it would be like having a whole bathful of water emptied over your head! And there's more wet weather on the way. In the afternoon, the sky turns purply black with towering thunderclouds. There's a flash of lightning and a crash of thunder and – hey presto! – a thunderstorm's on its way. Watch out, you're in for a serious soaking.

Horribly humid

Rainforests are horribly hot and sticky because of high humidity. That's the tricky technical term scientists use to talk about the amount of water vapour in the air. (Water vapour's water in gas form.) Warm air can hold more water vapour than cold air. That's why the rainforest feels so bloomin' sticky. It's humidity that makes you sweat like a pig and makes your clothes go horribly green and mouldy. You see, they never get a chance to dry out. So you'll look and smell *really* nice!

Teacher teaser

If all this has left you too worn out to drag yourself outside at break, try this scientific-sounding excuse. Put up your hand and say politely:

PLEASE, SIR, MAY I STAY IN? MY DAD SAYS I'M HYGROPHILOUS AND IT'S CATCHING

CATCHING!

Your teacher will be so flummoxed you might get away with it. But what on Earth is wrong with you?

Answer: Oh dear, going outside's the best thing for you, I'm afraid. How unlucky is that? You see, hygrophilous (high-gro-filus) is the posh word for a plant that grows outside where it's nice and humid and damp. Somewhere just like a bloomin' rainforest. And no, it isn't catching. But be careful *you* don't catch a cold!

OUT YOU GO!

Earth-shattering fact
If you set out to walk from one end of the Amazon rainforest to the other, it would take you at least a month. Even if you walked all night and day. You see, the Amazon's the biggest rainforest on Earth, by a very long chalk. It blooms along the banks of the awesome Amazon River in South America and covers an enormous six million square kilometres. That's almost as big as Australia. By rainforest standards, that's bloomin' huge.

A REALLY LONG WAY

A REALLY, REALLY LONG WAY!

Spotter's guide to rainforests

You might think all rainforests look the same but you get lots of different types. Trouble is it's tricky telling them apart because they've got so many things in common. For a start, all rainforests are hot and wet. They're all lush and green and steamy. And they're all bursting with amazing animals and plants. So how on Earth can you tell them apart? Well, it all depends where they grow. Still can't see the wood for the trees? Why not check out Fern's quick rainforest factfile and find your way out of the tangle?

1

Name: **LOWLAND RAINFORESTS**

Location: Low-lying land around the Equator

Forest features: These fabulous forests are hot and wet and packed with tall, evergreen trees (they're trees that stay green all year round). Some of these bloomers grow more than 45 metres tall and some, called "emergents" (they pop out of the top), can reach 90 metres. Their tops form a thick, leafy roof over the forest which botanists like me call the canopy. Lowland forests are teeming with plants and animals. Awesome, isn't it?

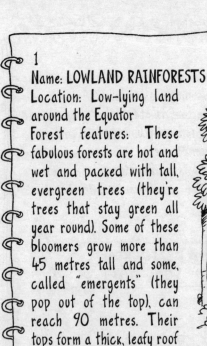

You'll get to know these forests better because they're what this book is mostly about.

Name: **MONTANE FORESTS**

Location: High up on tropical mountains or hills

Forest features: These hillside forests are cooler than those that grow lower down. And the higher you go, the colder it gets. They're dank, damp and covered in clinging cloud. (That's why they're also called cloud forests.)

I CAN'T SEE A THING!

They're the perfect place for hygrophilous (remember they're plants that like the heat and damp) bloomers such as mosses, lichens and ferns. They sprout in the gloomy undergrowth.

Name: **MANGROVE FORESTS**

Location: Along tropical coasts

Forest features: These are huge, muddy swamps where tropical rivers flow into the sea. They're named after mangrove trees. These unusual bloomers have long, tangled roots for gripping the mud as the tide tries to shift it. They've also got roots that stick out of the water like titchy snorkels for sucking in oxygen so the trees can breathe. Brilliant, isn't it?

Freaky fish skip about on the mud. You could say they're fish out of water, ha, ha! In fact, they're called mudskippers (howls of amazement!). The biggest mangrove forest stretches for 260 kilometres along the Bay of Bengal, between India and Bangladesh. But if you're planning a paddle, watch out for tigers — they love to gobble up fishermen.

Name: FLOODED FORESTS

Location: Along the banks of tropical rivers

Forest features: When a river bursts its banks, it floods the forest around it. The forest can stay underwater for months on end. The water rises by some 15 metres, drowning all but the tallest trees. It's tough luck on the birds and monkeys that live among the branches. They're left high and dry when their homes get flooded out. But it's great news for hungry forest fish. They swim among the underwater tree trunks, guzzling fruit and seeds.

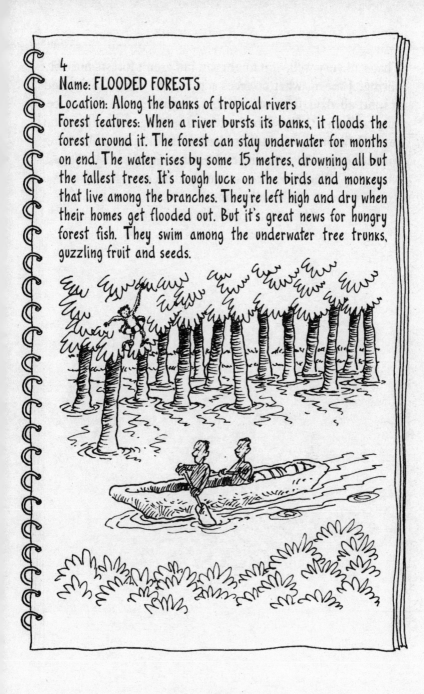

That's all very well, you might say, but aren't forests horribly boring? I mean, what do trees actually do, apart from stand around all day? It's not like you can take a tree for a nice, long walk, is it? You'd be better off getting a dog. But you couldn't be more wrong. The bloomin' rainforests are bursting with some horribly exciting and interesting plants. And guess what? Yep. There *is* even a tree that likes to go for walks. Read on if you don't believe me.

RAINFOREST BLOOMERS

The first thing you'll notice about the rainforest is all the bloomin' greenery. (Well, what did you expect?) It's like being inside a huge greenhouse, and I mean HUGE. The steamy rainforest heat's perfect for plants to grow all year round. And all that rain means they get loads of water to slurp. But you won't find boring tomatoes and prize dahlias growing in here. Not like the ones your grandad grows in his greenhouse. Oh no. Rainforest fruit and veg is far freakier than that. You'll find trees as tall as 20 geography teachers, flowers that reek of mouldy old cheese, and vicious vines that strangle their neighbours. Eek! Is that weird enough for you? Are you brave enough to sneak a closer look? Here's Fern to show you around.

A rainforest: the inside story

Well, here I am in the bloomin' rainforest, surrounded by fabulous foliage. It's heavenly! Anyway, before I get carried away, there are a few things you should know. The first is that rainforest trees grow in layers, depending how tall they are. Our tour starts right at the very top. What d'ya mean, you're not coming with me?

LAYER 1: EMERGENTS

I'M NOT TOO GOOD WITH HEIGHTS SO YOU'LL HAVE TO FORGIVE ME IF I GET A BIT... OOH! BEST NOT TO LOOK DOWN. I'M HERE AMONG THE TALLEST TREES IN THE FOREST AND WHEN I SAY TALL, I MEAN TALL. THEIR TOPS POKE OUT AT A SCARY 60m ABOVE THE GROUND. EACH TREETOP'S THE SIZE OF A SOCCER PITCH. SO WE'RE TALKING PRETTY BIG BLOOMERS HERE. BECAUSE THEY'RE SO TALL, THEY TAKE A BIT OF A BATTERING FROM THE HOWLING WINDS AND START TO SWAY. HELP! THEY ALSO GET STRUCK BY LIGHTNING. AND THEY'RE HOME TO MASSIVE MONKEY-EATING EAGLES. LET'S HOPE THEY DON'T EAT GEOGRAPHERS! JUST IN CASE, I'M OUTTA HERE!

LAYER 2: CANOPY

PHEW! THAT'S BETTER. KIND OF. THE THINGS I DO IN THE NAME OF GEOGRAPHY. THE CANOPY'S LIKE A HUGE, GREEN UMBRELLA OVER THE FOREST. HERE, THE TREETOPS MAKE A LUSCIOUS LAYER OF JUICY LEAVES ABOUT 6 m THICK, AND IT'S NICE AND WARM, THOUGH I'M ALREADY SOAKING WET. BUT THESE CONDITIONS MAKE A PERFECT HOME FOR THE RAINFOREST'S OTHER INHABITANTS, AND TWO THIRDS OF ALL THE FOREST PLANTS AND ANIMALS LIVE HERE IN THE CANOPY. SO IT'S A BIT CROWDED UP HERE, TO SAY THE LEAST. I THINK I MIGHT MOVE ON DOWN AND GET A BIT NEARER TO THE GROUND

LAYER 3: UNDERSTOREY

SMALL TREES, LIKE SPINDLY PALMS AND SAPLINGS, SPROUT DOWN HERE. NOT EXACTLY STRONG ENOUGH TO HOLD UP A GEOGRAPHER LIKE ME, SO I WON'T HANG AROUND. THEY GROW BEST IN GAPS LEFT WHEN OLD TREES DIE OR A STORM BLOWS THEM OVER. THAT GIVES THE SAPLINGS A CHANCE TO GRAB SOME OF THE SUNLIGHT. THE TREES HERE GROW ABOUT 15 m HIGH AND THEY'RE COVERED IN TANGLED VINES AND CREEPERS. TARZAN WOULD HAVE FELT RIGHT AT HOME. NOW WHERE'S THAT BLOOMIN' ROPE GONE? AAARGHHHH!

LAYER 4: FOREST FLOOR

AHEM, BIT OF A BUMPY LANDING THERE BUT NOTHING BROKEN, THANK GOODNESS. DOWN HERE, IT'S SO BLOOMIN' DARK AND GLOOMY NOTHING MUCH CAN GROW APART FROM MASSES OF DAMP-LOVING MOSSES, FUNGI* AND FERNS. (BRILLIANT FOR BREAKING FALLS.) THE GROUND'S LITTERED WITH OLD, DEAD LEAVES WHERE MILLIPEDES AND OTHER CREEPY-CRAWLIES LURK. (DID I TELL YOU I'M SCARED OF INSECTS? WELL I AM...) AND WATCH YOUR STEP. THAT BIT OF WOOD MIGHT LOOK LIKE A HARMLESS BRANCH BUT IT COULD BE A DEADLY POISONOUS SNAKE. HISSSSS!

* THAT'S WHAT BOTANISTS LIKE ME CALL THINGS LIKE MUSHROOMS, MOULDS AND TOADSTOOLS

Horrible Health Warning

You take your socks off after a hard day's hike, and shock horror! Your toes have gone all mouldy and green! Don't panic. In the steamy rainforest, things go off very fast. The gruesome green mould's actually a type of fungus that normally scoffs dead leaves and animal bodies from the forest floor. But they'll eat smelly feet too – lucky they're not fussy. The greedy fungi guzzle valuable chemicals from their food. Then, when they die and rot, the chemicals go into the soil. Which is great news for rainforest trees. Their roots suck the nourishing chemicals up and use them to grow. To cure your pongy problem, you need to let your feet dry out. Easier said than done.

Eight tree-mendous plant facts

Could you be a budding botanist like Fern? Turn your teacher green with envy with these tree-mendous plant facts. But be warned. Rainforest plants don't sprout in nice, neat, well-behaved rows like the roses and daffs in your dad's flower beds. These bloomers are green, mean and dangerous to know, and they grow like mad all over the place…

1 How many trees grow in a rainforest? Millions is the answer. It would take you years to count them all. Are you *really* that desperate to miss double geography? But you'd have trouble finding two trees the same. In a patch of rainforest the size of a soccer pitch, there may be 200 different types of tree. It might not sound much but in temperate forests (they grow in colder parts of the world), you'd be lucky to find ten.

2 Think of your house, with another nine houses balanced on top. That's how bloomin' high the tallest rainforest trees grow. To stop them toppling over in the wind, massive roots grow from their trunks and anchor the tree in the ground. The roots are a bit like the guy ropes that hold up a tent. Except that they can be an amazing 5 metres high – think how big that would make your tent!

3 Some plants can't reach the sun on their own. They have to hitch a lift on another plant. For instance, lianas are woody, jungle vines, as thick as a person's leg. They can grow 200 metres long and are strong enough to swing on. (Remember all those old Tarzan films?) A young liana grows roots in the ground, just like a normal plant. Then it winds itself round a nearby tree. As the tree grows, the liana grows with it up towards the sun. Simple as that.

4 Rainforest trees have to grow tall to reach the sun. But it's not because they want a suntan. You see, plants can't just pop along to the shops if they're feeling peckish. They have to make their own fast food and they need the sun to do it. Here's what they do…

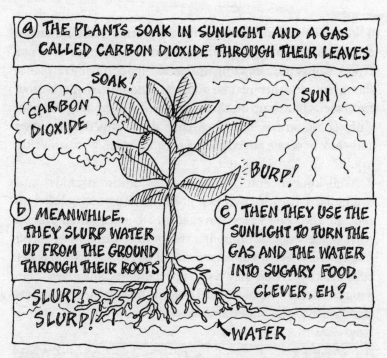

5 When a tree crashes down in the forest, it's bad news for forest floor plants. They get squashed flat. But that doesn't stop the amazing stilt palm. This ingenious bloomer sprouts stilt–like roots and walks away from the tangle. Yes, this is one plant you really *can* take for a walk.

6 Some plants don't bother with the ground at all. Botanists call them epiphytes (epi-fites). This comes from two old Greek words meaning "plants" and "upon". They're plants that grow on other plants, you see. These high-fliers grow from seeds blown up on the breeze or dropped in birds' poo. They settle on tree branches, then their roots dangle down and suck in water from the moist air.

7 Well-known epiphytes include exotic orchids and bromeliads (bro-mell-ee-ads). Bromeliads are related to pineapples. Their spiky leaves form a bucket which fills up with water when it rains. It's the perfect place for a forest frog nursery! What happens is this. The mother frog lays her eggs near by. When they hatch into tadpoles, she gives them a piggy-back to the bromeliad pond. The tadpoles eat insects that fall into the water and soon grow up into big, strong frogs. Aaah!

8 Competition for sunlight can be fierce in the forest. So some plants have dirty tricks up their leaves, sorry, sleeves. Take the sinister strangler fig, for example. This vile vegetable sprouts high up on a tree branch, then wraps itself around the trunk, tighter and tighter… Meanwhile, its roots dig into the ground and steal the tree's supply of water.

Slowly the foul fig strangles the tree and blocks out all its light. The tree dies and rots away, leaving a terrible trellis of fig roots behind.

Designer bloomers

No, they're *not* those giant knickers grannies often wear. You know the ones I mean! These bloomers are rainforest flowers. Not all rainforest flowers are sneaky and mean like the frightful strangler fig. In fact, some are sickeningly pretty and sweet. But their fabulous features aren't just for show. They're for impressing birds and other creatures for pollination*.

*Pollination is how flowers make their seeds. Flowers are filled with yellow dust called pollen. To pollinate, the pollen needs to shift to another flower of the same type of plant. Most rainforest flowers use animals to carry their pollen from one plant to another. Then the plant makes seeds that grow into baby plants. So, you see, pollination's pretty vital. Without it there wouldn't be any bloomin' rainforests at all. That's why flowers go to so much bother.

But first they need to grab the animal's attention. And for this they need to look GOOD. That means perfume, colour and designer flowers. Yes, the whole bloomin' works. What's in it for the animals, you might ask? Well, they get to nosh on tasty nectar – that's a sweet, sticky syrup flowers make.

But animals don't just find any old flower to visit. They're much pickier than that. Many flowers are exclusively designed for one particular type of creature. So, if you were a hungry hummingbird, which of these three designer bloomers would you head for?

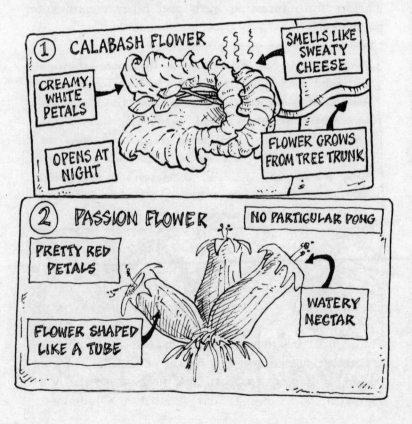

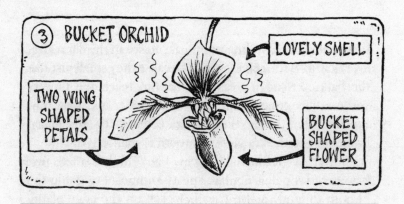

③ BUCKET ORCHID

LOVELY SMELL

TWO WING SHAPED PETALS

BUCKET SHAPED FLOWER

Answer:

2 These two are made for each other. Birds have excellent eyesight and like bright colours but they can't smell a thing. So there's no point in the flowers they visit having a strong pong. The hummingbird's long beak is brilliant for poking about deep inside flowers, before it slurps up the nectar with its long tongue. As it does this, pollen sticks on to its head.

By the way, hummingbirds may be tiny (some are only as big as bees!) but they've got truly gigantic appetites. To keep up, you'd need to scoff about 130 loaves of bread a day – that's more than 1,000 rounds of cheese sandwiches. Burp!

In case you were wondering, the perfect pollinator for **1** is a bat. Bats are nocturnal (that means they fly about at night and doze during the day) and that's when this clever flower blooms. It's white so it's easy to see in the dark. Bats love flowers with a cheesy pong because they smell just like the bats do. And it's easy for bats to reach the flowers because they grow straight out of the tree trunk. That way, the bats don't snag their delicate wings on the sharp branches and there's plenty of room to manoeuvre.

Flower 3 is pollinated by bees. They think it smells just heavenly. Its petals act like spotty signposts to guide the bees in to land. A bee tries to perch on the edge of the bucket but it's horribly slimy and slippery. The bewildered bee loses its footing and tumbles in with a splash! The bucket's full of water. Is there any escape? Yes, but it isn't easy. The bewildered bee has to force its way up a narrow tunnel inside the flower and out of a side door. But not before two big blobs of pollen have landed on his back. Splat!

Say it with flowers

Have you noticed how flowers do strange things to people? How they make even geography teachers go all gooey-eyed? Desperate to get into *your* teacher's good books? Why not say it with a big bunch of rainforest flowers? Only NOT these freaky blooms. They're definitely not to be sniffed at. To find out how *not* to get up your teacher's nose, pop into Auntie Fleur's Freaky Flower Shop.

Welcome to Auntie Fleur's Freaky Flower Shop, petals. You'll find flowers for every occasion in here. Even quite smelly and unpleasant ones. Here are four of my own particular favourites...

NAME: RAFFLESIA
WHERE IT GROWS: BORNEO, SUMATRA, INDONESIA

APPEARANCE: GIANT ORANGE-BROWN BLOOM SHAPED LIKE A SCHOOL CABBAGE. LEATHERY PETALS COVERED IN WARTS. IT'S THE WORLD'S BIGGEST FLOWER, GROWING UP TO A METRE ACROSS.

THE BLOOMIN' DETAILS:

① IT GROWS INSIDE THE ROOTS OF RAINFOREST VINES AND SUCKS OUT THEIR LIFE JUICES.

② IT'S ALSO KNOWN AS THE "STINKING CORPSE LILY" BECAUSE IT REEKS OF ROTTING FLESH. PHWOAR!

③ ITS PUTRID PONG ATTRACTS FLIES FOR POLLINATION. THEY THINK IT'S A TASTY MEAL. OH DEAR.

If you want to say it with flowers, I'd stick to roses, if I were you. Unless you're buying it for someone you really don't like. I mean, it's not like they'll ever talk to you again.

45

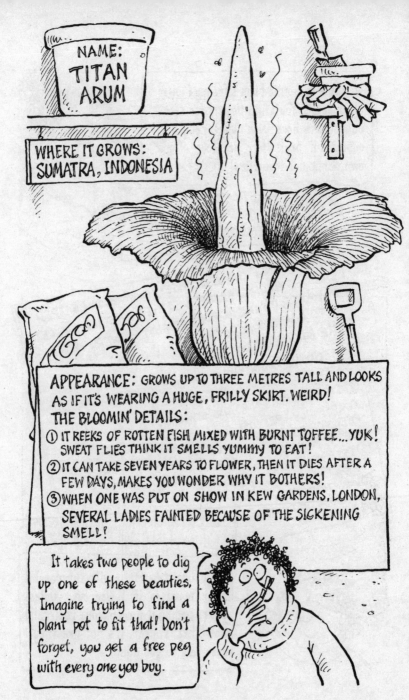

NAME:
TITAN ARUM

WHERE IT GROWS:
SUMATRA, INDONESIA

APPEARANCE: GROWS UP TO THREE METRES TALL AND LOOKS AS IF IT'S WEARING A HUGE, FRILLY SKIRT. WEIRD!

THE BLOOMIN' DETAILS:

1. IT REEKS OF ROTTEN FISH MIXED WITH BURNT TOFFEE...YUK! SWEAT FLIES THINK IT SMELLS YUMMY TO EAT!
2. IT CAN TAKE SEVEN YEARS TO FLOWER, THEN IT DIES AFTER A FEW DAYS, MAKES YOU WONDER WHY IT BOTHERS!
3. WHEN ONE WAS PUT ON SHOW IN KEW GARDENS, LONDON, SEVERAL LADIES FAINTED BECAUSE OF THE SICKENING SMELL!

It takes two people to dig up one of these beauties. Imagine trying to find a plant pot to fit that! Don't forget, you get a free peg with every one you buy.

NAME:
TROPICAL
STINKHORN FUNGUS

WHERE IT GROWS:
SOUTH AMERICA

APPEARANCE:

LONG, SLIMY SPIKE COVERED IN WHITE, LACY VEIL.

THE BLOOMIN' DETAILS:

1. THIS FREAKY FUNGUS REALLY LIVES UP TO ITS NAME. IT REEKS OF ROTTEN MEAT AND SMELLY TOILETS.

2. FOREST FLIES FLOCK TO THE FUNGUS TO GUZZLE ON THE DISGUSTING SLIME. MEANWHILE, THEIR BODIES GET DUSTED WITH SPORES (TINY SPECKS THAT FUNGI GROW FROM).

3. SOME RAINFOREST FUNGI GLOW IN THE DARK. EVEN THE EXPERTS DON'T KNOW WHY. IT MIGHT BE FOR SCARING OFF HUNGRY BEETLES THAT LIKE TO NIBBLE THE FUNGI AT NIGHT.

This bloomer's really lovely to look at. An excellent choice for birthdays and Christmas. If you want your house to smell like a cesspit and swarm with flies, that is.

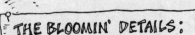

NAME: PITCHER PLANT
WHERE IT GROWS: AFRICA, SOUTH EAST ASIA, SOUTH AMERICA, AUSTRALIA

THE BLOOMIN' DETAILS:

1. AN INSECT LANDS ON THE RIM OF THE PITCHER, LOOKING FOR YUMMY NECTAR TO DRINK. BUT IT'S IN FOR A NASTY SHOCK. IT SLIPS ON THE WAXY SURFACE AND PLUNGES INTO A POOL OF WATER INSIDE. THERE'S NO ESCAPE. THE PLANT SQUIRTS OUT DIGESTIVE JUICES TO DISSOLVE ITS BODY. THEN IT SOAKS ITS VICTIM UP.

2. SOME PITCHER PLANTS LOOK LIKE TRUMPETS, CHAMPAGNE GLASSES AND LANTERNS. THERE'S EVEN ONE SHAPED LIKE A TOILET. COMPLETE WITH TOILET LID!

3. THE BIGGEST PITCHER PLANT IS THE RAJAH PITCHER. ITS FOUL FLOWER CAN HOLD A BUCKETFUL OF WATER AND TRAP VICTIMS AS BIG AS MICE.

Well, they say pride comes before a fall. But if pitchers are your cup of tea, and there's no accounting for taste, don't forget you'll need a good supply of fresh flies to feed your fiendish flower with.

Earth-shattering fact
Durian fruit reek of rotten fish but they taste delicious.
Especially to orangutans. These awesome apes love slurping
the yummy custard-like flesh inside. They're too busy stuffing
their faces to spit out the seeds. Later they have a poo and the
seeds plop out. (Better not mention these disgusting details
while you're having tea with your squeamish old aunt.)

Which is great news for the durian tree. It means its seeds get
scattered around the forest so they can take root and sprout.
What's more, the seeds get a nice, big dollop of orangutan poo
fertilizer to help them grow big and strong!

Scandalous seeds

You might think flower seeds are pretty harmless and spend
their lives quietly growing into new plants. You probably
wouldn't expect a humble handful of seeds to cause a
shocking scandal. But believe it or not, they did. The seeds
in question were rubber-tree seeds. Read on and discover
the whole shocking story.

A rubbery discovery
Rubber trees grow in the South American rainforest. Their
posh scientific name is *Hevea brasiliensis*, in case you were

wondering. Rubber's actually made from the milky juice, or latex, that oozes out when you cut slits in their bark.

And it's horribly useful. You can turn it into loads of useful things, like car tyres and rubber bands. And you can use it to rub out mistakes when you're doing your geography homework. What's more, it's cheap and easy to grow. No wonder horrible humans saw rubber as a way to get rich, quick.

The first European to see wild rubber trees was posh French explorer and scientist, Charles Marie de la Condamine (1701–1774). (Of course, local people had known about rubber for years. They used it for making bouncy rubber balls and waterproofing their canoes.)

In 1743, Charles sailed down the Amazon River on a raft and wrote a book about his adventures. Among the things he wrote notes about were getting a painful shock from an electric eel and seeing his first rubber tree. He even made a rubber carrier bag for his things and sent some bits of rubber home as souvenirs.

When news of de la Condamine's discovery reached Europe, it caused a massive stir. You see, apart from being able to bounce, rubber was brilliant for keeping things dry. Scottish scientist, Charles Macintosh, used rubber to make wellington boots and raincoats snug and waterproof. (That's how macintoshes got their name.) Then an American inventor, Charles Goodyear, worked out how to make rubber into tyres for the recently invented car. There was no looking back. Soon rubber was all the rage. Trouble was, it only grew in far-off Brazil where trade was controlled by wealthy businessmen called rubber barons. No doubt they were rubbing their hands with glee.

Young British botanist, Henry Wickham (1845–1928) soon put a stop to all that. In 1876, the government hired him to smuggle some rubber-tree seeds out of Brazil. Henry jumped at the chance. After all, he'd got nothing better to do.

He collected 70,000 rubber seeds and packed them into crates, carefully wrapped in banana leaves. Then he hired a ship to carry his precious cargo back to Britain.

If anyone asked, Henry pretended he needed the seeds for the royal plant collection at London's Kew Gardens. Otherwise, the authorities would never have let him leave with his illegal booty. Luckily for him, they believed his excuse and he and the seeds reached home safely. Back at Kew Gardens, nearly 7,000 of the precious seeds sprouted into tiny rubber trees. These were packed off to Sri Lanka and Malaysia to grow on huge plantations. Within a few years, there were millions of trees, producing millions of tonnes of cheap rubber a year. The Brazilian rubber barons were ruined.

As for Henry, he was paid £700 for his trouble and given a knighthood. But the scandal surrounding the stolen seeds never died away. Some people said he'd done a great service for his country. Others accused him of being a petty plant criminal. Today, this kind of plant pilfering would never be allowed. Fed up with all the fuss, Henry moved to Australia to try his hand at growing tobacco and coffee. But he ended up losing all of his money in a shady deal. Poor Henry never really bounced back. What a bloomin' shame.

But plants aren't the only things lurking in the rainforest undergrowth. Ever get the feeling you're being watched? Well, you are! It's time to meet some seriously shady characters. If you dare…

SHADY CHARACTERS

Picture the scene. It's mid-afternoon in the rainforest. You've got the freakiest feeling you're being watched. But apart from the odd, lonesome lizard, there's no one else around. Weird. A lot of the animals on the planet live in the bloomin' rainforest. So where on Earth are they all? You might not be able to see them but they're there, believe me. The thing is, many of these shady characters are nocturnal. That means they doze all day and come out at dusk for the night shift when they hunt for food. (Other animals are out and about during the day and go to sleep at night. That way, there's always plenty of food to go round.) Others are just plain shy. So you have to use different ways of finding out when an animal's about. But here's an amazing fact. The most common animals in the rainforest aren't big brutes or hairy beasts. They're incredible insects and other ugly bugs.

Scientists who study insects are called entomologists (ent-o-moll-ogists). They get their name from an old Greek word for "cut up". This is because an insect's body looks like it's been "cut up" into three. Guess how entomologists find out about insects? Yep, they chop the insects up. (I expect the insects were pretty "cut up" about that!) Anyway, I'm sticking to flowers. All this talk about insects is giving me the creeps.

Ants in your pants

Lift any mossy old stone in your garden and chances are some creepy-crawly will scurry out. Look in any dark nook or cranny and you're bound to disturb a spider. But guess where you'll find more insects than anywhere else on Planet Earth? Yep, in the bloomin' rainforest. Shake any rainforest tree and a staggering 1,500 different types of insects might come fluttering out. It's true.

Entomologists have counted at least one million types of rainforest insect but there may be millions more out there. Most of them are tiny but they're capable of some outsized feats. Take awesome ants, for starters…

1 How many types of ants live in one rainforest tree? Give up? The answer's about 50. This might not sound very much to you but you'd only find 50 in the *whole* of Britain. Multiply that by millions of rainforest trees, and that's an awful lot of ants. In fact, scientists think ants account for a third of all rainforest creatures. And they get absolutely everywhere from inside plants to inside your pants. Mind you don't get bitten!

2 Leaf-cutter ants are seriously small fry. But they're also immensely strong. These incredible insects can lift 50 times their own body weight in leaves. That would be like a human weight-lifter picking up an elephant. Now that *would* be awesome.

3 Leaf-cutter ants cut up leaves and carry them back to their underground nest. They chew them up and mix the bits with droppings and spit to make a compost heap. Then they grow fungus on it to eat. The house-proud ants keep their gardens neat and tidy and pull out any unwanted weeds.

4 Tailor ants make their own cosy tree nests from leaves stitched together with silk. But they don't use needles and thread for sewing. That would be too boring. They use their own ant grubs instead, passing them backwards and forwards between two leaves.

THIS IS GIVING ME A HEADACHE!

Meanwhile, the adult ants give the grubs a gentle squeeze to get the silk flowing from their mouths. Thank goodness your parents don't do this to you!

5 Some plants have their own pet ants living inside their stems and leaves. Azteca ants live inside the trunks of trumpet trees. The ants take a store of tiny insects along and live off sugary juices these insects make. So the ants get a safe place to shelter and plenty to eat. But what's in it for the patient plants? Well, Azteca ants can't sting but they've got a horribly painful bite. Which makes them brilliant bodyguards. Anyone who comes near their tree-house gets well and truly nipped. Then the angry ants squirt acid into the wound just for good measure! Ouch!

6 If you thought these awful ants were appalling, think again. In the jungles of South America lurks an even angrier ant than that. And it'll have you running for your life! Trouble is, this fierce creature doesn't travel alone.

It's part of an awesome army, at least 20 million ants strong. This terrifying troop marches through the forest, devouring anything daft enough to get in its way. It strips frogs, snakes and even birds to skeletons. Very creepy! But army ants can be horribly useful, believe it or not. They raid people's homes and gobble up cockroaches and other insect pests. Don't worry, the horrible humans get well out of the way first. Byeee!

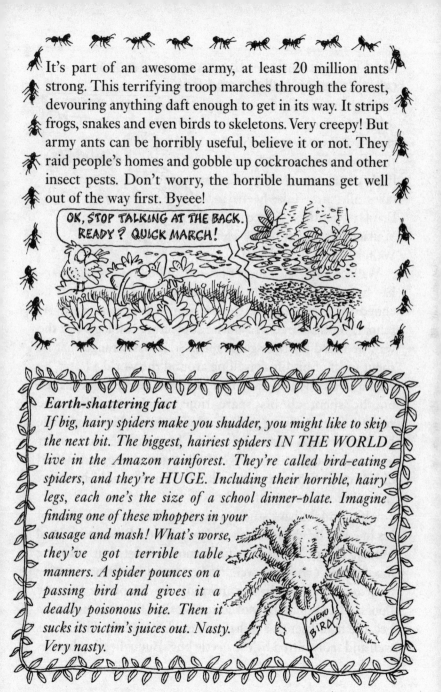

OK, STOP TALKING AT THE BACK. READY? QUICK MARCH!

Earth-shattering fact
If big, hairy spiders make you shudder, you might like to skip the next bit. The biggest, hairiest spiders IN THE WORLD live in the Amazon rainforest. They're called bird-eating spiders, and they're HUGE. Including their horrible, hairy legs, each one's the size of a school dinner-plate. Imagine finding one of these whoppers in your sausage and mash! What's worse, they've got terrible table manners. A spider pounces on a passing bird and gives it a deadly poisonous bite. Then it sucks its victim's juices out. Nasty. Very nasty.

MENU BIRD

Mad about beetles – the amazing Amazon adventures of Wallace and Bates

Creepy-crawlies do strange things to people. Some people can't even spy a spider without shrieking with fear. Other people find them fascinating. Yes, it takes all sorts. Take beetle-mad British scientists, Alfred Russel Wallace (1823–1913) and Henry Walter Bates (1825–1892)…

Wallace and Bates didn't set out to be famous scientists. Far from it. In fact, Alfred started off as a teacher but he ended up preferring beetles to pupils. I wonder why? At school, young Alfred's favourite subject was biology. (By the way, he hated horrible geography. So it was strange that he spent most of his life travelling around the world.) Later, he read a book about botany that changed his life. From then on, he spent all his spare time wandering about the countryside, studying and sketching plants. He even made his own pressed flower collection. Very pretty. No wonder his brother called him a weed. But green-fingered Alfred didn't care. Whatever anybody else might think, he knew that greens were good for him.

Alfred might have stuck to pressing flowers for the rest of his life. But by chance he met Henry Walter Bates in his local library. Henry was a part-time entomologist, but studying insects didn't pay very well. So he earned his living working in a local brewery. In the morning, he swept the brewery floors. After lunch, he looked for beetles. The two men soon became firm friends and before very long weedy Alfred was well and truly bitten by the beetle bug. But collecting beetles in Britain was dead boring. There just weren't enough new ones around. It was time for curious Wallace and Bates to spread their butterfly net a bit wider. They'd read about the Amazon rainforest in another library book which called it "the garden of the world". And where better to hunt for brand-new beetles than in a truly gigantic garden? They decided to take a tropical trip to the awesome Amazon. It was horribly exciting.

Wallace and Bates arrived in Belem, Brazil in May 1848, on board a cargo ship called *Mischief* after a journey lasting a month. Both men stood blinking in the bright tropical sunshine. Neither of them looked like an intrepid explorer at all. Alfred was pale, gangly and horribly short-sighted. Henry was tall, thin and painfully shy. But looks aren't everything. Without even stopping for a well-earned rest, the two men stocked up with supplies, hired some local guides and a canoe and set off into the jungle. Despite the heat, the flies and the damp, it was like a dream come true. Here's how Alfred described his first sight of the forest:

"I could only marvel at the sombre shades, scarce illuminated by a single direct ray of the sun, the enormous size and height of the trees . . . the extraordinary creepers which wind around them, hanging in long festoons from branch to branch."

What's more, it was like being in insect heaven. They'd never seen anything like it before. There were beetles and butterflies everywhere. Wallace and Bates were soon busily beetling away, collecting insect specimens which they pickled or pinned on to cards. Their plan was to ship them back to England where a museum had promised to pay them threepence a piece. Which might not sound much until you know that Henry alone collected 14,712 different types of insects (8,000 of which scientists had never seen before – they got horribly excited)! So he really earned his money. Every day, Henry worked from 9 a.m. to 2 p.m., with a short break for lunch. Here's how he described a typical day in a letter to his brother:

Over my left shoulder slings my double-barrelled gun. In my right hand I take my net; on my left side is suspended a leather bag with two pockets, one for my insect box, the other for powder and two sorts of shot. On my right hand hangs my "game bag", an ornamental affair, with red leather trappings and thongs to hang lizards, snakes, frogs, or large birds. One small pocket in this bag contains papers for wrapping up delicate birds. To my shirt is pinned my pin cushion with six sizes of pins.

But this trip was to be no picnic. On their jungle travels, Alfred and Henry were driven mad by mosquitoes, shot at by unfriendly locals and laid low by life-threatening fevers. Once, a whopping anaconda snake attacked their canoe. It bored a hole in their chicken coop (they'd brought the chickens along for food) with its head and made off with a couple of chickens.

But worse was to come. In August 1852, Alfred decided he'd seen enough of the rainforest for now and set sail for home. Halfway into the voyage, disaster struck. The ship he was sailing in burst into flames and sank, taking Alfred's precious collection of specimens down with it. All poor Alfred's diaries and sketches were lost, apart from some notes about palm trees and some drawings of fish. Alfred himself only just made it back alive. He was finally rescued after spending two weeks adrift at sea.

It was a serious setback. Devastated and broke, Alfred returned to England but he didn't stop his life's work. It wasn't long before he was back among his beloved beetles, this time in South-East Asia. In just eight short years, he collected a staggering 125,000 specimens, including beetles, butterflies and birds. What happened to Henry, you might ask? Well, he spent several more years in the Amazon before heading home to write a book. OK, so it was boringly called *A Naturalist on the River Amazon* but it was so horribly gripping and exciting it became a bestseller. So, for the first time ever, Wallace and Bates put rainforests (and their weird and wonderful wildlife) well and truly on the map. Which was great news for budding geographers everywhere.

How *not* to get eaten alive

Brave Wallace and Bates lived to tell the tale but other rainforest creatures aren't so lucky. Many jungle animals scoff plants for their tea. So it's a good job there's so much greenery. But some vicious creatures have more sinister eating habits. Forget fruit and veg. Their favourite meals are … each other! Amazingly, some cunning creatures manage to get away and even turn the tables on their attackers. So if you don't want to end up as elevenses, how on Earth do you do it? If you want to find out how jungle animals stay alive, why not take a peek at this essential Survival Manual. It's been put together by an old friend of Fern's, Major Ray N Forest and it's full of sneaky survival tactics.

Chameleon

OK, so this is a tough one. But to all you chameleons out there, let's hope you've got plenty of colours in your paintbox because you're going to need them. I know you're normally green and brown but all

that's got to change! Do you hear me? I'm not talking a bit of fawn here, or beige there. I WANT TO SEE CAMOUFLAGE! And I want to see it fast. Yes, in a matter of minutes, you need to change colour to blend in with whatever background you're up against. That way, your enemies won't know where to find you. But you've gotta be ready for action. I mean, this ain't no game of painting by numbers!

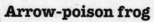

Arrow-poison frog

Now, my little friend, just because you're small doesn't mean you don't have to bother. I know you like wearing bright colours on your skin and, granted, they're good for warning your enemies off. I mean, they're really LOUD! But you need more than that. I'm talking poison. I want your slimy skin to ooze deadly juices. Those dudes ain't gonna touch you again, once they get a skinful of that! There's just one problem. Some human hunters might try to roast you over a fire. Don't panic, they don't want to eat you. They want to sweat the poison out of you so they can make poison arrows.

Orchid mantis

You don't fool me. I know you look like a harmless flower but you're a tricky customer all right. I don't think you need me to teach you anything in the way of self protection. Even your wings sway in the breeze just like delicate petals. Very cunning, I give you that. But I know how deceptive appearances can be. Any insect that lands on this bloomer is in for a nasty shock. I've seen you in action, and it ain't pretty. Quick as a flash, you grab the insect and bite its head off. A class act if ever I saw one.

Jaguar

I know, I know. You're the fiercest hunter in the rainforest so why should you listen to lil ol' me. But WISE UP, my friend, and don't let pride come before a fall. You need to keep your wits about you. Yeah, I'm talking to you! OK, so you've got a fur coat to die for which hides you among the dappled forest light. But I want you to be careful. When you're sneaking up on prey, take cover in the undergrowth, then pounce. It's the first rule of laying an

ambush. Then you're on your own but with claws like yours, no one's gonna try stealing your supper.

False coral snake

I'm not saying this one's a yellow-belly but when it comes to rainforest survival, you don't have that much to hand. Go on, admit it, you're completely harmless! But fair's fair, give respect where it's due. If this fella can fool everyone into thinking it's poisonous, that's fine by me. You do a pretty good impression of a true coral snake which is deadly poisonous. You've even got the same dashing red, black and yellow colours to warn away the enemy. A brilliant avoidance tactic. (You just have to hope no one sees through your disguise.)

OOPS!

Horrible Health Warning
Eating hairy, poisonous caterpillars is bad for your health. (Even school dinners aren't that dangerous.) At best, you'll break out in an itchy rash. At worse, you might be dead. Here's how the golden potto (a small furry animal like a bushbaby) from Africa gets round this prickly problem. It sniffs out a caterpillar (they smell terrible), then bites it on the head. Then it rubs the ghastly grub between its hands to break off its deadly hairs. It gobbles the caterpillar down then wipes its face clean on a branch.

YUM! YUM!

On the move

If you don't have your own poisonous hairs, you could always try running away. If you can't run fast, you could fly, or glide, or climb the bloomin' trees instead. This is handy for escaping from enemies and for sneaking up on prey. Time to meet some of the niftiest movers in the rainforest…

ANIMAL OLYMPICS

Running Winner: The basilisk lizard can walk on water. It's true. So how on Earth does it do it? Well, it slaps its long, webbed back feet on the water so fast it doesn't fall in. A brilliant way of crossing ponds and rivers if you can't swim!

Climbing Winner: Tiny tree frogs live high up in the rainforest canopy. They've got minute, sticky suction pads on their fingers and toes. The sure-footed frogs can climb straight up a tree  trunk, and even hang upside down from a leaf, without falling off. Bet you don't know anyone who could do that.

Flying Winner: While they're sipping tasty nectar, hummingbirds hover in front of flowers like teeny helicopters. But they have to beat their wings about 90 times a second to stay in the air. That makes the humming sound you can hear. These nifty movers can even fly backwards. Hmmmm…

Swinging Winner: Gibbons are kings of the rainforest swingers. These acrobatic apes hurl themselves through the trees at top speed. Luckily, they've got extra-long arms with extra-long fingers and toes for  grabbing hold of the branches and they can cover 10 metres in a single bound. To match this, you'd have to swing right across your classroom. Now mind where you land.

Gliding Winner: The handsome paradise flying snake can't really fly but it does the next best thing. It glides through the air at high speed. But it doesn't have wings. Instead it launches itself from a tree, then flattens out its body. It floats down to land on a branch like a long, thin parachute.

Could *you* be a three-toed sloth?

What's green and hairy and hangs around in a tree? No, it isn't your teacher's long-lost woolly cardy.

Give up? The answer is the strange–looking sloth that hangs out in sultry South America. Believe it or not, this appalling animal's even more bone idle than you are. Even the word "sloth" means lazy. Try mentioning that to your mum when she's trying to drag you out of bed. But which of the sloth's filthy habits are too revolting to be true? Try this quick quiz to find out. Mind you don't nod off now…

1 A sloth spends 18 hours a day sleeping. TRUE/FALSE?
2 A sloth's so filthy its fur turns green. TRUE/FALSE?
3 A sloth only comes down to the ground once a week. TRUE/FALSE?
4 Sloths are slower than tortoises. TRUE/FALSE?
5 Scientists who study sloths are always falling asleep. TRUE/FALSE?

Answers:
Believe it or not, they're all TRUE. Sloths really are that bloomin' lazy. Like you, their idea of a perfect day is sleeping, eating, not combing their hair and not having a bath. Yawn! But what's wrong with hanging around in the canopy doing nothing all day? The sleepy sloth doesn't care. Sorry, are we keeping you up? Zzzzz!
1 Even when a sloth isn't asleep, it doesn't shift very far.

It might crawl slowly along a branch, chomping on some leaves. But that's as far as it goes. Awake or asleep, the sloth always hangs upside down in the trees. It holds on with its vice-like claws so it never drops off to sleep, ha! ha! Even its horrible hair hangs upside down so the rain drains off.

2 Normally a sloth has shaggy brown fur but it gets so disgustingly dirty that small plants start sprouting on it. This is what turns it ghastly green. (Actually, this green colouring's horribly useful for hiding the sloth amongst the trees from enemies such as jaguars.) And if that's not horrible enough for you, masses of minute moths crawl about in the sloth's festering fur, munching on the plants.

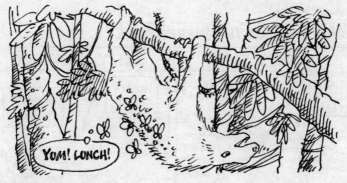

YUM! LUNCH!

3 Once a week, the sloth leaves its tree … but only to go to the toilet. It has a poo in a hole on the ground then climbs back up again. Meanwhile, the moths fly out of its fur and lay their eggs in the steaming pile of poo. When the grubs hatch, they scoff the sloth poo. Nice! Soon afterwards they turn into adult moths and find a sloth of their own to live on.

4 Even at top speed in the trees, a sloth only crawls along at a sluggish 0.2 kilometres per hour. That's about 20 times slower than you staggering to school. Compared to this slow-coach, tortoises are speedy movers. On the ground, sloths are even slower. Their legs are too weak and feeble to walk very far (it's the lack of exercise) so they drag themselves along on all fours. Strangely, sloths are brilliant at swimming. Not that most sloths ever go near water. In case you were wondering, they do breast-stroke or front crawl.

5 Scientists who study sloths have a tough time keeping their eyes open. I wonder why! Imagine watching a green, furry creature doing nothing for hours on end. It'd be worse than counting sheep. No wonder the first scientists to see a sloth weren't very polite about it. "I have never seen an uglier or more useless creature," one stupefied scientist said.

CAN YOU SPOT THE DIFFERENCE?

But before you head off for a good night's kip, WAKEY! WAKEY! Your jungle journey isn't over yet. Far from it. Forget sleepy sloths and plate-sized spiders. Someone else is waiting to meet you in the next chapter. Someone who could teach you a thing or two. (And no, it's not a geography teacher.) But make sure you mind your Ps and Qs with these rainforest residents…

JUNGLE LIVING

Despite the weird wildlife and the wet weather, about 1.5 million people live in the bloomin' rainforests. And they've lived there for thousands of years. They rely on the forest for everything – their food, clothes, homes and medicines. You name it, it's found in the forest somewhere. In return, they treat the rainforest with great respect, making sure they don't do it any harm. Sounds like a great way to live, you might say. But don't be fooled into thinking it's easy. Rainforest living can be horribly hard. I mean, when you're feeling peckish, what do you do? Drag yourself out of your armchair and chomp on a bag of crisps? You definitely *don't* have to set off into the forest to search for something to eat. Think you could hack some real jungle living? Ready to find out how rainforest people really survive? Who better to ask than the Yanomami people of South America. They know the rainforest like the backs of their hands...

My rainforest life by Yarima

My house and family

Hello, my name is Yarima. I live in the rainforest in Brazil, South America. I'm ten years old and I'm a Yanomami. That's what my people are called. My family lives in a village called Toototobi which is quite close to the river. It's a beautiful place to live. All the people in my village live together in a huge house built in a clearing in the forest. There are about a hundred of us in all. The house is called a yano and it's built in the shape of a giant circle. Our yano's made of wood from rainforest trees and it's got a thatched roof made from palm leaves. It's cool in the day and warm at night. Perfect! My dad and the other men in the village built this yano a few years ago. Inside, each of the families has its own fireplace. We hang our hammocks around the fire and that's where we sleep. The fire keeps us warm at night and keeps the mosquitoes away. It's also where we do our cooking. My pet monkey likes to curl up in my hammock with me. I've also got a pet toucan and lots of dogs. I'm really lucky. In the middle of the yano, there's a big space that's open to the sky. That's where we play and have meetings and parties. I love living in the yano. Apart from my mum, dad and brothers, my grandparents, aunts, uncles and cousins all live there, too. So we're one great big family. There's always someone to talk to or play with or look after you when you're ill. OK, so we fall out and squabble sometimes but we never get bored or lonely.

My day

I get up early in the morning, as soon as the sun comes up. Then I go to the river with the other girls to wash. It's fun splashing each other and diving in. Then we go home and have breakfast. It's usually manioc bread* dipped in pepper sauce or an avocado. After breakfast, we go to school in the yano to learn to read and write. We learn our own Yanomami language and also Portuguese so we can talk to people who live outside the forest. School only lasts for a few hours so it's not too bad. Afterwards we go swimming in the river or climb the trees. Then we have to help our mothers with the chores.

My brothers and the other boys go off with the men to learn how to hunt in the forest. Sometimes they're away for several days, camping in the forest. The men catch monkeys, wild pigs, armadillos and tapirs with their bows and arrows. Sometimes they go fishing in the river. They stand in a canoe and catch fish with their spears. It's very difficult. The boys watch and practise hunting lizards. My brother can't wait to grow up and go hunting for

74

real, even though it can be horribly dangerous. Last week, my uncle was badly hurt when a wild pig charged at him. And sometimes they don't catch anything, which is very bad news for us and we get very hungry.

Yanomami girls like me don't go hunting. I help my mother collect firewood and water. It's very hard work! I also help look after our little garden where we grow manioc, bananas, peanuts and peppers. Sometimes my mum and I go into the forest to collect Brazil nuts, caterpillars and peach palms. And I'm learning to make my own hammock. But it's taking a long time.

My mum and dad are brilliant! They teach us about the forest and about the animals and plants that live there. We learn which plants are good to eat and which can make us ill. They teach us to love the forest because it gives us everything we need to live. My dad says, "Each time you cut down a tree you must ask its forgiveness or a star will fall out of the sky." We also learn to be generous and share what we have with other people. That's very important to the Yanomami people.

I've been feeling very sad lately because my mum's been really ill. She feels very tired and has a fever. All she wants to do is sleep.

My dad says she has the flu - that's a sickness brought to the forest by the goldminers. My dad says people sometimes die of flu and Mum needs special strong medicine. But we don't have any of that. I don't want my mum to die.

A great feast

In the evening, the men come back from the forest and share out the food they've caught. Sometimes we sit around the fire after dinner, telling stories about the forest. Sometimes we have a big party to celebrate a good day's hunting. There's singing, dancing and a huge feast. People come from the villages all around to join in the fun. It's a really exciting time for our village. My friend Marta and I get ready by painting our faces and bodies red and black with coloured dyes made from plant juice. We wear bright green and yellow parrot feathers in our ears. There's loads of delicious food to eat. But the best news is that my mum's feeling loads better and after the feast tonight, my mum and the other women started singing songs about the forest. My friends and I love joining in. We sing songs to thank the forest spirits for giving us enough to eat. We believe that the spirits live in every forest plant and animal. If we make them angry, they can make us ill or take the animals away so we don't have any food. So we have to keep them happy!

The party goes on until late at night but my mum says I've got to go to bed. Tomorrow there's going to be a big meeting in the yano to talk about the illness Mum had. Dad says we've got to do something to stop the goldminers making us sick and harming the forest. I hope we don't have to leave the forest. I love my home.

Come on, monkey, time for bed. Goodnight, everyone.

Manioc's a vegetable a bit like a potato. Rainforest people make it into bread and beer. But first they have to pound it into a pulp and squeeze the juices out. Otherwise it's horribly poisonous. If you ate it raw, you'd have had your chips and that's for sure!

Teacher teaser

Feeling brave? If you want to see your teacher turn crimson with rage, crush up some seeds from the urucu plant, mix them with water and use the paste to paint your face.

But why is your teacher seeing red?

Answer: Because she's just seen your ugly mug, that's why. You see, the urucu paste turns your skin bright red. The Wai Wai people of South America deliberately paint their faces with it to avoid being ambushed by evil spirits. The Wai Wai don't think spirits can see red. So what's your excuse? The Wai Wai also paint their pet dogs red so the sinister spirits can't spot them either. Besides, the pungent paste's great for keeping mosquitoes away.

DID YOU MISS THE BUS AND HAVE TO RUN TO SCHOOL?

Fruits of the forest

If you're going to live like a rainforest local, you'd better get used to the food. You might think school dinners taste disgusting. And, of course, you'd be right. But be warned. Forget soggy cabbage and lumpy custard. Check out this revolting rainforest restaurant instead. Some of the dishes on the menu might leave you feeling a teeny bit green. Are you ready to order? Go on, tuck in.

Revolting Rainforest Menu

STARTERS

- **Freshly boiled grasshopper garnished with ants.**
  Make sure you cook the ants for at least six minutes to get all the poison out.
- **Roasted palm grubs on sticks.**
  Eat the grubs whole or split them open and suck out their juicy insides.
- **Delicious hot fruit soup.**
  Made from freshly picked forest fruits, such as soursop, rambutan and durian (despite their strong smell, you can eat the lot), simmered in herb-flavoured water. Pick out anything that looks like small oranges – they're deadly poisonous strychnine fruits.

MAIN COURSE

- **Chef's special rainforest stew.**
  Made from fresh cuts of monkey, tapir and wild pig, and perhaps a bat or two. Boiled until it's soft and tender to chew.
- **Succulent capybara steaks with barbecued banana.**
  Not suitable for guinea pig owners. Capybaras are huge rodents that look like gigantic guinea pigs. They taste like a cross between pork and fish. Apparently.
- **Freshly caught piranha fish.**
  Mind your fingers on their nasty sharp teeth. Served with a side dish of roasted tarantula.

PUDDING

- **Slice of fresh honeycomb.**
  Tastes delicious but is horribly risky to collect. First you have to climb a tall tree and stick your hand into a bees' nest. You'll have a bunch of smoking leaves to fend the bees off but chances are you'll still get stung.

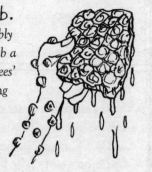

Could you be a rainforest hunter?

If you're hiking through the forest and your stomach starts rumbling, what on Earth can you do? You can't just pop along to the shops. There aren't any shops to pop along to! Feeling brave? You'll need to be. You're about to go hunting for your supper. What do you mean you've gone off your food? Don't worry, you'll be in good company. The Mbuti people of Africa are expert hunters. Stick with them and they'll show you what to do...

1 You pitch camp in the forest. The Mbuti are nomads. This means they move from place to place in search of food. They don't stay anywhere long, just until supplies run out. So they don't need especially hard-wearing homes. Instead, they put up small, round huts

WHERE'S THE TENT? WHERE'S THE SLEEPING BAGS?

made from bent-over branches and leaves. Just right for keeping the rain out. And they're handy because they only take two hours to build.

2 Next day, you wake up at dawn. You light a fire to honour the forest and ask for its blessing on the hunt. After breakfast of roast bananas and rice, you set off into the forest. Traditionally, the Mbuti use large nets and spears for hunting. (Other rainforest locals use bows and arrows, or long blowpipes instead. Today, some use shotguns. Trouble is, the noise of the guns being fired scares the animals away.) The nets are made from super-strong forest vines and can last for years and years.

3 You follow an antelope's tracks through the forest. (The Mbuti also hunt monkeys, snakes and wild pigs.) The Mbuti are expert animal trackers. They know exactly where to go. But ssshhh! You don't want to frighten the animals off or let them know you're coming. So you'll have to walk on tiptoe over the dry, crunchy leaves. The Mbuti can do this without making a sound. Question is, can you?

4 Just then, you spot a group of antelopes grazing among the trees. But don't say anything, whatever you do, or you'll scare them away. Instead, you'll have to make a special hand signal to tell the others what you have seen.

WHAT'S THE HAND SIGNAL FOR ANTELOPE?

5 You hold out your net with the other hunters to make a big semicircle shape. Meanwhile, some of the villagers hide among the surrounding trees. Then suddenly they rush forward and shoo the antelopes into the nets. The hunters kill the antelopes with their spears which they've dipped in deadly poison.

6 You carry the antelopes back to the camp and cook them over the camp-fire. Everyone gets a share of the roast meat. There are baskets of freakily-named forest mushrooms to go with it. Everyone enjoys a feast. Afterwards, you sing and dance around the camp-fire to thank the forest for giving you a good day's hunting.

Mary Kingsley's fang-tastic adventure or "One For The Pot"

But head-hunters weren't the only hazard you'd have faced in the past. Losing your head was one thing, but what about ending up in a cannibal's cooking pot? What a horrible thought. Mind you, this didn't stop plucky English explorer, Mary Henrietta Kingsley (1862–1900). You could say brave Mary stepped out of the frying pan straight into the fire…

Mary had a miserable childhood. Her dad was often away from home and her mum was always ill and Mary had to look after her. When Mary was 30 years old, both her mum and dad died. With nothing to keep her at home anymore, daring Mary decided to set off for Africa to study how the local people lived. Her friends thought she was barmy. For a start, she'd never been to Africa. In fact, she'd never been abroad before. Besides, at that time, travelling alone in a strange country wasn't a very ladylike thing to do. Did Mary care? Did she, heck. She spent a happy year exploring in Africa and if anyone asked her why she was there she had a brilliant excuse. She said she was searching for her long-lost husband and, luckily, it did the trick. But that was just the start of Mary's adventures. The following year she was off again.

The British Museum in London asked her to collect some specimens of rare river fish that were only found in Africa. There was just one teeny problem. The bits of Africa the fish were found in lay deep in the bloomin' rainforest and were horribly risky to reach. So risky that no outsiders had ever been there before. What's more, they were home to some particularly fierce and unfriendly cannibals, alarmingly called the Fang. Most people would have said no, fang-you, and told the museum to find their own bloomin' fish. But Mary was much more daring.

Did Mary live to tell the tale? Or did she end up in very hot water? Here's what one of her letters home might have looked like.

The Ogowe River, Gabon, Africa
July 1895

My dear brother, Charles,
I hope this letter reaches you safely. I'm sorry I haven't written for a while but I've been rather busy, you see. And what a week it has been. You know I'm here collecting fish for the museum? Well, I headed off down the Ogowe in search of some really rare specimens. The first part of the journey was brilliant. I caught a paddle-steamer which was most pleasant and comfortable, I must say. Trouble was, it couldn't go over the rapids so I had to change ships and go on by canoe. What a palaver. We capsized a couple of times and once a crocodile tried to climb on board. (I gave it

a good whack on the nose with a paddle and it didn't bother us again.) The leeches are far worse, though. What loathsome creatures they are. Once they get a grip on you, there's no shaking them off. Luckily, I'd packed a pair of your old trousers so I popped them on under my skirt. That made my legs nice and leech-proof, at least.

Anyway, I hired five local men as guides and soon we reached the Great Forest between the Ogowe and Rembwe rivers. That's the jungle to you and me. It was so exciting to be here at last after reading about it in books. Do you know, I'm the first outsider ever to come here? Isn't that exciting? Eventually we reached a Fang village called Efoua where I was lucky enough to find a room. Now, Charles, I know what you're thinking, dear. The Fang are fearsome cannibals who eat intruders for breakfast and I was bound to end up in the cooking pot. But, you know, they've been very good to me so far. I paid my way with some cloth and fish hooks and I've never been frightened at all. Besides, you know my favourite motto, "Never lose your head".

Mind you, yesterday I got the shock of my life. There was a very odd smell in my hut, sort of sweet and sickly like rotten fish. I sniffed around a bit and it seemed to be coming from an old cloth bag hanging on a hook on the wall. What a stink! I'm afraid to say my curiosity got the better of me and I opened the bag and emptied it into my hat. I made sure no one was watching, first. I didn't want to offend them.

Anyway, you'll never believe what was in it — a human hand, three big toes, four eyes and two ears! Yes, dear, ears! The hand actually looked quite fresh. I later learned that, even though the Fang are rather partial to eating people, as you feared, they always keep a bit of their victims as a souvenir. It's rather gruesome, I admit, but fascinating, don't you think? But Charles, please don't worry about me. I'm still in one piece. Besides, I've got my little revolver tucked in my boot in case things turn nasty.

We're off to another Fang village tomorrow, though the guides aren't very keen. They're convinced they're going to be boiled alive. We shall see. Then I'm off to climb Mungo Mah Lobel (Mt Cameroon). I've never climbed a mountain before, it's really exciting. But I should be back in good time for Christmas, dear.

Your loving sister,
Mary

PS By the way, I collected 65 brand-new types of fish. Brilliant, isn't it?

BRILLIANT

Mary returned to England in December and immediately became a star. She wrote a best-selling book about her travels and was invited to give lectures and talks to geographical societies. She even had three of the fish she'd found named after her. But her story has a very sad ending. In 1899 she went to South Africa to nurse wounded soldiers and died the following year.

Local people have lived in the rainforest for thousands of years. But today their lives are changing. The forest is being chopped down around them and they're being forced to leave their homes. Many have died from diseases such as malaria, measles and flu. These are brought in by people who come to settle in the forest from outside. Some local people are trying to fight back and protect the forest. Otherwise their ancient way of life may die out. And that would be a terrible tragedy.

BUDDING EXPLORERS

Some people have horribly itchy feet. But it's got nothing to do with wearing the same smelly socks for days. Truth is, they simply can't sit still. Take intrepid explorers, for example. You wouldn't catch them sitting around all day, glued to the telly. No, they were always setting off for far-flung places where no outsiders had set foot before. Perilous places like deadly deserts and terrifying mountain peaks. Oh, and bloomin' rainforests, of course. So why on Earth did they do it and why do they still set off today? Some wanted to trade in forest treasures such as spices, timber or gold. They were in it for the money. But others were horrible scientists and geographers. They simply wanted to see the world. And their curiosity made them do strange and unexpected things…

Rambles through the Amazon rainforest

Posh German geographer, Alexander von Humboldt (1769–1859), hated school. He wanted to see the world. But to please his mum, he went off to university and got a dead boring job in the Department of Mines. He spent most of the day deep underground, but at night he headed off into the countryside. You see, Alexander was potty about plants.

In 1796, Alexander's mum died. So he set off on his travels. He resigned from his job and learned map-reading in case he ever got lost. Then he teamed up with top French botanist, Aime Bonpland (1773–1858).

Aime trained as a doctor but he much preferred plants to his human patients. Does that make him "barking" mad? Anyway, the two men got on like a house on fire and soon became firm friends. They signed up on a five-year expedition to explore the South Pole where their knowledge of science might come in useful. But at the last minute the trip was called off. Bitterly disappointed, Aime and Alexander walked from France to Spain instead. And there their luck changed. By chance, they met the King of Spain who gave them permission to visit South America. (At that time, South America was ruled by Spain and you needed the king's say-so to go there.) For our heroes, it was like a dream come true. In the South American rainforests, they could study plants to their hearts' content. But it wasn't going to be easy...

Where better to read about their amazing voyage than in these extracts from Alexander's jungle journal? His real journal was much, much longer than this because Alexander made notes about everything — but you get the idea. And he was always amazingly chirpy and cheerful, even when things went horribly wrong.

89

My Jungle Journal (short version)
by
Alexander Friedrich Wilhelm Heinrich Humbolt (Baron)

July 1799, Cumana, Venezuela

We sailed from Spain on 5 June. I couldn't believe it. We were off at last! Yippee! Hooray! Look out, world, here I come! I'm so excited, I could burst. The voyage was really brilliant. We spent a few days in Tenerife and climbed an (extinct) volcano. Fantastic. Then the journey proper began. On the way, I took lots of samples of sea water and algae (tiny plants). Then disaster struck. Half the ship's crew went down with typhoid, a dreadful disease. We headed for the nearest port – Cumana in Venezuela (in South America) which is where we are now. Still, every cloud's got a silver lining. Of course, it's terrible for the sick men and I hope they get better but what a bloomin' ace place this is! There's so much to see and do. I don't know where to begin. Trees with monster-sized leaves and huge flowers, and animals and birds everywhere. Heaven!

February 1800, Caracas, Venezuela

We've been here since November. It's the rainy season, you see, so it's far too wet to travel. But there's no time to get bored. We've been sorting out all the specimens we've collected so far – there's hundreds of them! Once the weather turns drier, we'll travel south to the Orinoco River. Apparently, there's a stream called the Casiquiare linking it to the mighty Amazon. I can't wait.

March 1800, almost at the Orinoco River, Venezuela
What a month! We set off from Caracas on horseback with our trusty local guides. But riding across the river plains was hell. Even I found it hard to keep smiling. We thought we'd suffocate in the baking heat, die of thirst or be eaten alive by bugs. Still, mustn't complain. We've reached the rainforest at last, in good health and good spirits considering what we've been through. We travel all day, then pitch camp on the riverbank. We hang our hammocks in the trees around a blazing fire. Lovely!

The guides catch fish for supper while Bonpland and I write our diaries up. It's really rather cosy. The fire also helps keep jaguars at bay. You can hear them roaring away in the dark. Scared? Not me. Jaguars are just big pussy cats! Aaaaghhh! What on Earth was that?

1 April, 1800, the Orinoco River

We've swapped our horses for a canoe and we're paddling up the Orinoco. Into the unknown. What a thrill! But it's bloomin' hot, I can tell you. Luckily, our canoe's got a little thatched hut at the back to keep the sun off. It's stuffed full of plants and animal cages (mostly full of parrots and monkeys) so it's a bit of a squash if we get in. Tra! la! la! la! Tra! la! la! la! Messing about on the river...

4 April, 1800, further up the Orinoco

Phew! What a narrow squeak. We stopped near a thick patch of jungle. I was bursting to go off and explore. What a place! What plants! What animals! What a paradise on Earth! Ahem. Sorry, got carried away. Anyway, I stopped to investigate a freaky fungus on the forest floor, and then I looked up ... straight at a jaguar! Shivers ran down my spine. What on Earth was I to do? Then I remembered a useful piece of advice that someone once gave me: "Should you meet a jaguar, just turn slowly and walk away. But don't look back."

And that's exactly what I did. Very slowly, I turned my back and walked away. At any moment, I expected the creature to pounce. Then I'd have been a goner. Luckily for me, when I dared turn round, the jaguar had disappeared. It must have eaten already.

PS I take back what I said about pussy cats.

May 1800, the Casiquiare River

At last, we've found the Casiquiare. And not a moment too soon. It's been pretty hard going, even for me. Crossing the rapids in a flimsy canoe was frightening enough. But what really bugged us was the mosquitoes. We slapped on rancid alligator fat to keep those irritating insects off. It smelt terrible and it didn't do much good. Still, I'm trying to stay cheerful, despite it all. Poor Bonpland's not quite so chirpy. He's been bitten all over, and his face is all puffed up and covered in blisters. Oh, and we're down to eating our last few ants and some dried cocoa beans. I suppose it's better than nothing.

A few days later, Esmeralda

Funny how such a terrible place can have such a pretty name. Still it hasn't been a complete waste of time. I've conducted a very exciting experiment. The local people told me they use a deadly poison called curare to tip their hunting arrows. It's made from the bark of a jungle vine. And it can kill a monkey (or human) in minutes. But it's only fatal if it enters your bloodstream. Apparently. Well, you know me, I love a challenge. So I swallowed some to see. OK, it was risky but guess what? I'm still here! Luckily.

93

To cut a seriously long story short…

Alex didn't have to wait long for his next trip. As soon as poor old Bonpland was on his feet, the two were off again. For the next four years, they hacked through rainforests, squelched through swamps and scaled more violent volcanoes. Back home in Europe, they were treated like superstars, particularly Alexander. He had hundreds of places named after him, including a crater on the Moon. Why? Well, no one had ever made such a long journey simply for horrible geography's sake. What's more, Alex's real diaries were crammed with valuable notes and sketches of places, people and wildlife never seen before.

Horrible rainforest holidays

What's the worst holiday you've ever had? The one when you lost your luggage or when it poured with rain? Don't worry. You're in bloomin' good company. The unfortunate travellers you're about to meet have some truly terrible tales to tell about holidays from hell. Would *you* go on holiday with any of this lot? On second thoughts, you might be better off staying at home. Here's Fern to introduce you to them…

NAME: Isabela Godin (1729-1792)
NATIONALITY: Peruvian
HOLIDAY FROM HELL:

French explorer, Jean Godin, thought he'd booked the holiday of a lifetime when he set off down the Amazon in 1749. He was going back to France after years exploring the rainforest. His patient wife, Isabela, stayed behind until he could fetch her. Little did she know, it would be another 20 years before she saw her holidaying husband again. But Isabela wasn't to be put off. She finally grew tired of waiting and set off on her own on one of the worst holidays ever known. One by one, her travelling companions ran away, or drowned, or died from hunger and disease. Soon only plucky Isabela was left. Half-dead, she struggled on alone, eating roots and insects. The food was terrible! Luckily, some friendly locals helped her reach the coast. And guess what? A few weeks later, against the odds, Isabela and Jean were reunited. It might have been a holiday from hell but it had a happy ending!

95

NAME: Charles Waterton (1782–1865)
NATIONALITY: British
HOLIDAY FROM HELL:

South America is one of the world's most exotic holiday hotspots. As Charles Waterton found out. He made several trips there to find types of jungle animals. Let's just say he enjoyed adventure holidays. He shot the animals and stuffed their skins so that he could study them at leisure. But it was horribly risky work. Dare-devil Charles once captured a boa constrictor alive by wrestling it to the ground and tying its jaws up with his braces. He also rode on the back of a giant alligator, using its front legs as reins. Back home, he set up a nature reserve to put all his weird wildlife and holiday mementoes in.

NAME: Richard Spruce (1817–1893)
NATIONALITY: British
HOLIDAY FROM HELL:

Top botanist Richard Spruce enjoyed the sort of holiday where you plan your own itinerary. He spent years collecting thousands of new types of Amazon plants, mapped miles of rivers and learned to speak 21 local languages. So he didn't need a holiday rep to help him do his souvenir shopping. But it wasn't all plain sailing. Several times, Richard nearly died from malaria. Another time he woke up to hear his guides plotting to kill him in his sleep. Luckily, he managed to talk them out of it, proving that it was a good idea to learn a little of the local languages. It's always appreciated.

NAME: Benedict Allen (born 1960)
NATIONALITY: British
HOLIDAY FROM HELL:

There are some holidays that only the most adventurous traveller should dare to take on. Benedict Allen was just such a holidaymaker. In the 1980s, he spent months in the Amazon rainforest, travelling by foot and dug-out canoe. No luxury air-conditioned coach for this intrepid explorer. The trouble started when his local guides left him and he lost his canoe. For a month he struggled alone, eating only dried soup, fried locusts, nuts and ... dog! Yep, he finally had to kill and eat his pet dog. But, despite nearly dying from a fever, plucky Benedict made it out alive. We say: well done, Benedict, for being our bravest holidaymaker so far!

Could you be a budding explorer?

Just imagine if you were lost in the rainforest. How on Earth would you survive? Would you know how to shake off a poisonous snake or make friends with a blood-sucking leech? Try this life or death survival quiz to find out how you'd do. But be careful. With all the horrible hazards about, it's a bloomin' miracle anyone gets out alive. What's that? You'd rather do extra homework than risk your neck in there? Must be bad. You'd better send your geography teacher to the rainforest instead. And don't let him peek at the answers...

1 You're in the steamy rainforest and you're dying for a drink. Trouble is, there's very little water around, despite all the rain. Which plant can help you quench your thirst?

a) A vine.

b) A bromeliad.

c) A pitcher plant.

2 It's night-time and you're nodding off to sleep. Then something large, black and SCARY flaps by. It's a vampire bat and it's after your blood. How do you avoid being bitten?

a) Snore very loudly. It'll scare the bat off.

b) Stop watching so many late-night horror films. Vampires aren't real, silly.

c) Wrap yourself up in a mosquito net, even if there aren't any mosquitoes around.

3 Help! Another blood-sucker's taking a liking to you. This time it's a loathsome leech. Talk about making your skin crawl! If a leech sucks up to you and sinks its jaws into your leg, how on Earth do you get rid of it?

a) Pull it off.

b) Wait till it's full of blood, then it'll drop off.

c) Sprinkle salt on it.

4 Watch your step. There's a gigantic log blocking your way. At least, it looks like a log, but is it? In the rainforest, things aren't always as harmless as they seem. Remember the murderous orchid mantis? Just in case the log's *actually* a poisonous snake, what should you do? After all, you don't want to put your foot in it, do you?

a) Step on it … gently.

b) Pick it up and throw it away.

c) Poke it with a stick.

5 You've been walking for miles. You're all hot and bothered and you feel as if you're about to faint. You're not sure you can go any further. What should you eat to make you feel better?

a) A banana.

b) Some salt.

c) A chocolate bar.

Answers:

1 a), b) and **c).** All three would do the trick. But be careful. If you're getting water from a vine, make sure you choose the right one. Some vines are horribly poisonous. Here's how you can tell. Cut the vine with a knife. If the liquid that pours out is clear and doesn't burn your mouth, it's perfectly safe to drink. If it's cloudy, red or yellowish and stings, steer clear. Make sure you strain water from bromeliads or pitcher plants first to get rid of the creepy-crawlies.

2 c) The bats can't nibble you through the net. Phew! But keep your nose, fingers and toes safely tucked inside. These are the bits beastly bats love best. Whatever you do, try not to snore. It tells the bloomin' bats where to find you. Vicious vampire bats attack their victims at night while they're sleeping. Apart from snoring humans, they also attack cows, horses and pigs. They nip your skin with their razor-sharp teeth, then lap up your blood. The strange thing is you won't feel a thing because their spit numbs the pain. Then the bloated bats return to their roost and sick up some of the blood for their batty relations. Vile.

3 b) and **c)**. Leeches live on the damp forest floor. Like vampire bats, they feed on blood. They sink their teeth into your skin, then slurp until they're full.

Don't try to pull a blood-sucking leech off, whatever you do. They've got sticky suckers at either end and they'll cling on for dear life. Wait until their vile bodies are full of blood, then they'll simply drop off. (This may take some time – a thirsty leech can slurp five times its own weight in blood. IN ONE SITTING!) Or sprinkle them with salt or sugar. This'll make them shrivel up and die. You have to be cruel to be kind. Better still, tuck your trousers into your socks and wear a pair of long socks on top. It won't look very cool but the leeches will loathe it!

4 a) Step on the log, *very* gently. If it ups sticks and slithers off, it's probably a snake. Never ever poke a snake with a stick. If you want to stay alive. Some deadly poisonous snakes lurk on the rainforest floor. And they're horribly hard to spot. Some look exactly like fallen logs or piles of leaves.

But don't be fooled. Mess with one of these beauties and you'll be sorry. Dead sorry. Take the bushmaster snake, for instance. If a bushmaster bites you, you'll be dead in hours. First you start sweating and throwing up, then you get a splitting headache. Eventually you lose consciousness. Your only hope is to get yourself along to a doctor fast.

5 b) You'll sweat buckets in the rainforest because it's so bloomin' steamy and hot. Trouble is, sweat's mainly made from water and salt, and you need both to stay alive. Lose too much of either and you'll feel feverish and weak. Then you'll feel dizzy and tired, and eventually, you'll get delirious and die. A very nasty way to go. The best thing to do is dissolve some salt in water and sip this, slowly. You might fancy a nourishing banana later, when you're feeling better. But forget the chocolate – it'll melt in the heat. Rainforest people keep cool by not wearing much but you (or your teacher) should cover up well. Long sleeves and trousers will stop you getting badly bitten and scratched.

Now add up your teacher's score...
Feeling generous? Award your teacher 10 points for each right answer.

Score: 0–20. Oh dear! Your teacher won't last long in the rotten rainforest. He's just too bloomin' green. At this rate, he'd be eaten alive before you could say "Watch out, there's a crocodile!" Wouldn't that be a pity?

Score: 30–40. Your teacher's got what it takes to be a budding explorer if he keeps his wits about him. But hang on... What are those two little bite marks on his neck? Aaaggh! He's been bitten by a blood-sucking bat!

Score: 50. Bloomin' marvellous. Your teacher's survived and he'll be back at school in no time. What's more, he'd make a brilliant rainforest explorer. Compared with teaching you, coping with loathsome leeches and sinister snakes will be easy peasy!

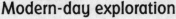
Modern-day exploration

Bored of sitting around all day, playing computer games? As if. Still, if it's a life of adventure you're after, why not head for the rainforest yourself? After all, you don't want your teacher getting big-headed, do you? For years, rainforests had horrible geographers stumped. They were desperate to sneak a peak in the canopy but it was just too bloomin' high up to see. Today, there are lots of ways of travelling through the treetops. Got a good head for heights? You'll need one where you're going...

Modern scientists and geographers head for the rainforests to study the wildlife and find out how the place works. They use ropes and harnesses to climb the tallest trees. They pinched the idea from mountaineers. They fire a fine rope over a branch on the end of an arrow, with a stronger rope tied to the end. They tie it on tightly, then haul themselves up. To get about from tree to tree, they use light metal walkways and ladders over 100 metres above the ground. (You'll soon get used to the swaying.) That's like popping out for an afternoon stroll on top of a 30-storey building. Freaky, or what?

You could also hitch a lift in a hot-air balloon or grab a ride in a cage dangling from the end of a massive crane.

SOFA, SO GOOD

If all this sounds like horribly hard work, you could always haul a comfy armchair up with you. That's what one bone-idle geographer did.

Yikes! Feeling dizzy? Better not look down. Of course, you could always keep your feet on the ground and monitor the rainforest by radar or satellite instead.

The good news is that there's still plenty of bloomin' rainforest left for budding geographers like you to explore. The bad news is it might not be around for long. All over the world, rainforests are being cut down and burned at an alarming rate. So if you're planning a visit, you'd better get your skates on...

FACING THE AXE

Bloomin' rainforests were once a lot bigger than they are today. And I mean *a lot*. They used to cover about a third of the Earth. Today there's less than half of this left. Sad to say, all over the world, precious rainforests are for the chop. So why are rainforests in deadly danger? Who's to blame? The bad news is that *we are* – horrible humans. Truth is, we're putting terrible pressure on the fragile rainforests and the rainforests can't fight back. Once the forests have gone, they can't grow back. Pretty depressing, isn't it? So why on Earth are rainforests going up in smoke? We sent Fern to get to the root of the problem...

Going up in smoke

So what's happening to the bloomin' rainforests, then?

They're being chopped down, that's what. Then some of the trees are burned to a cinder. So thousands of precious plants and animals go up in flames. Then the bulldozers move in...

Oh dear. Is this happening very fast?

Yep, it is. Unfortunately. Horrible geographers don't know exactly how rapidly rainforests are disappearing but it's at a truly alarming rate. Some experts estimate that a patch of forest the size of 60 football pitches is chopped down EVERY MINUTE. That's a chunk the size of Switzerland EVERY YEAR. Put another way, in the time it takes you to read this page, about 40,000 rainforest trees will have gone for good!

At this rate, how long will the rainforests last?

Not long is the alarming answer. Some geographers think there'll be no rainforests left in just 30–50 years' time. This might sound like a horribly long time to you but it's nothing to an ancient rainforest. After all, they've been around for millions of years. Already, tropical islands like Madagascar and the Philippines have lost 90 per cent of their forest cover. And there's not much forest left in Asia or Africa.

So why are rainforests for the chop?

Good question. But guess what? Like most things in geography, there isn't a nice, straightforward answer. Here are some of the worst culprits:

• **Logging.** *About half the rainforest is being chopped down for the timber trade. You see, valuable tropical trees like mahogany are worth thousands and thousands of pounds. The timber's sold to people in rich countries to make posh furniture, doors and windows, loo seats, coffins and chopsticks. Trouble is, the heavy machines used to cut the trees down damage the forest for miles around and hundreds of other trees are wasted.*

• **Gold mining.** *Some rainforests are rich in precious metals and gemstones such as gold, silver and diamonds. And greedy humans can't wait to get rich quick. But the*

chemicals they use to get at the gold are making the rainforest rivers seriously dirty. So fish and plants can't survive. Not to mention rainforest people who rely on the rivers for water and food. And to make matters worse, the miners build roads to take them and their massive machines to work, ruining vast stretches of forest.

• *Farming. Millions of people are moving out of crowded cities and into the rainforests. They clear plots of land to build houses and grow crops. But rainforest soil is quite thin and poor and the goodness is soon used up. Which means the people have to pack up, move somewhere else and start all over again. Local people have done this for years but they only clear smallish patches of forest. And they leave the land plenty of time to recover in between. But with so many new farmers to cope with, the forest can't take the pressure.*

• *Cattle ranching. Next time you tuck into a tasty hamburger, spare a thought for where the meat came from. Chances are it's from the rainforest far away in South America. Every year, huge stretches of forest are being cleared for beef cattle to graze on. Then the cattle are sold for their meat. Turning the bloomin' rainforest into fast food. Problem is, the grass they graze on sucks the goodness from the soil, leaving it dry and dead. Then the cattle are moved on.*

Mmm, I see. But would it really matter much if the rainforest went?

You bet it would. If the rainforests go up in smoke, so do millions of amazing plants and animals. They're killed or lose their homes. Experts think that at least 100 types of animals and plants are being wiped out every single week. And extinction is for ever. Nothing can ever bring them back. Among the animals on the brink is the beautiful Spix's macaw (a macaw's a bigish parrot). There's only one lonely Spix's macaw left in the wild (another 40 live in zoos). Parrots are also captured and sold for pets. It's against the law but it's tricky to stop. Other animals in danger include orangutans, jaguars, birdwing butterflies... Sadly the list goes on and on.

And that's just for starters. Closer to home, here are six other things you wouldn't have if the rainforests went up in smoke. (What d'ya mean, you didn't know they came from the forest in the first place?) Without bloomin' rainforests, you'd miss out on...

1 Brazil nuts: Yes, those festive nuts you crunch at Christmas grow on bloomin' rainforest trees. But mind your teeth. They're tremendously tough nuts to crack. They grow in hard shells inside huge pods, as big as cannonballs. You get juicy bananas, pineapples, oranges and lemons from the rainforest too.

2 Chocolate: Yummy choccy's made from the beans of the cocoa tree which grows in the rainforest. You know those chocolate coins you get at Christmas? The ones in little glittery string bags? Well, until about 150 years ago, in Mexico, real chocolate beans were used as money.

3 Chewing gum: Didn't know that chewing gum grows on trees? Well, it does. It's made from the juice of the rainforest chicle tree. You cut slits in the bark and the sticky goo oozes out. It's boiled up until it goes thick, then shaped into blocks. Tasty mint and fruit flavours are added later.

4 Vanilla ice cream: OK, you'd have the ice cream but not the tasty vanilla flavouring. It's made from the sun-dried pods of an exotic rainforest orchid. But vanilla's not the only succulent spice in the rainforest. There's also the pepper you put on food and the ginger in scrummy ginger biscuits.

5 House plants: Offer to water your mum's best pot plants, then take a good, long look at them. Chances are some of them are rainforest bloomers. Cheese plants, rubber plants, African violets and nasturtiums might look at home on the mantelpiece but they originally grew wild in the jungle.

6 Cane furniture: Cane's used to make baskets, mats and comfy armchairs. But it starts off as a woody rainforest vine. Its real name is rattan but it's also called the "wait-a-while" plant because once it sinks its sharp thorns into you, it takes you a while to break free again. Local people use strips of rattan as toothbrushes but they snap the spines off first.

Miracle medicines

Brazil nut choccies and ice cream might taste scrummy but you could live without them. Honestly! Some other rainforest bloomers could actually save your life. About a quarter of all the medicines we take when we're sick are made with plants that grow in rainforests. And scientists think there's loads more vital, live-saving veg just waiting to be discovered. Veg that could cure killer diseases like cancer and AIDS.

Of course, local people have used these marvellous medicines for years. And scientists hope that by finding out more about their usefulness they'll be able to save the rainforests. But could you be a rainforest plant doctor? Look at the list of symptoms below. Then try to pick the correct plant cure. On second thoughts, some of these plants are deadly poisonous except in very small doses. You might kill the patient you're trying to cure. Better leave it to an expert, like our very own Doc Leaf.

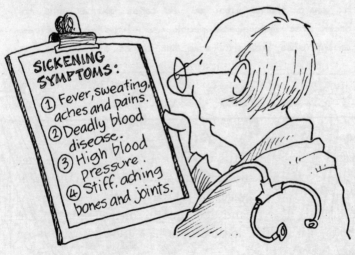

SICKENING SYMPTOMS:
① Fever, sweating, aches and pains.
② Deadly blood disease.
③ High blood pressure.
④ Stiff, aching bones and joints.

a) CALABAR TREE, AFRICA

b) CINCHONA TREE, SOUTH AMERICA

c) YAMS, MEXICO

d) ROSY PERIWINKLE, MADAGASCAR

Answers:
1 b) The bark of the cinchona tree contains a drug called quinine. The bark's stripped off and made into medicine which is used to treat the deadly disease malaria. It's spread by murderous mosquitoes and kills millions of people each year.

2 d) This brilliant little bloomer contains chemicals that doctors can use to treat the killer disease leukaemia. That's a type of cancer of the blood. It's already saved thousands of lives and doctors only discovered it in the 1950s. (Of course, local people had known about it for years.)

3 a) The beans from this rainforest tree can help to lower your blood pressure and treat glaucoma (that's a type of eye disease that can make you go blind). But in Africa, they were traditionally used to decide if a person was guilty. How? Well, if the suspect ate them, and survived, he or she was thought to be innocent. Sounds simple, doesn't it. Trouble is, the beans have a deadly secret. On their own, they're horribly poisonous. So whether or not you were really innocent, you could well end up being dead.

INNOCENT, INNOCENT, INNOCENT, GUILTY...

4 c) A yam looks a bit like a potato but this vital veg isn't used to make lumpy mash. Medicines made from Mexican yams are used for treating painful diseases of the bones and joints like arthritis and rheumatism. However, they have to be prepared very carefully. In large amounts, some yams can be poisonous.

People in peril

You might not think it when your mum's moaning at you for being late for school or you can't do your homework (again) but you're dead lucky. At least when you come home from school, your home's still bloomin' standing! Rainforest people aren't so bloomin' fortunate. They rely on the forest for everything – their homes, food and their livelihoods. And they lose them all when the forest's cut down.

Take the plight of the Penan people. They've lived in the Borneo rainforest for hundreds of years. Traditionally, they wander from place to place in search of animals to hunt and food to gather. They believe the forest is sacred and treat it with great respect. After all, they say, they are part of the forest and the forest is part of them.  But today, the forest is being chopped down for timber and their lives have been turned upside down. Many have been forced to leave the forest and settle in permanent homes far away. For the wandering Penan, it's like being in prison. The Penan people are trying to fight back to save their precious forest. But it's a terrible struggle. When they block the roads to stop the loggers, they're sent to prison or fined. What's more, many are dying from deadly diseases like malaria and flu brought into the forest by loggers. It's a desperate situation. For the Penan and many people like them, the future looks pretty bleak.

Horrible weather warning

Scientists say chopping the rainforests down is making the world's weather worse. How? Well, when the trees go up in flames, they spew tonnes of carbon dioxide gas into the atmosphere. (It also comes from cars and factories.)

This acts like a giant blanket around the Earth. It traps the heat coming from the sun and keeps the Earth snug and warm. Too snug and warm.

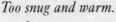

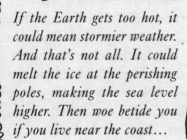

If the Earth gets too hot, it could mean stormier weather. And that's not all. It could melt the ice at the perishing poles, making the sea level higher. Then woe betide you if you live near the coast...

HELP!

Fatal floods are another worry. The rainforests act like giant sponges. You know, like that squishy yellow thing you soap yourself with in the bath but on a gigantic scale. The sponge-like trees soak up the rain through their roots and leaves. What's more, their roots bind the fragile rainforest soil together. Chop down the trees and there's nothing to suck up the heavy rain. It floods the land and flows into rivers, making them overflow. Before you know it, you've got a furious, full-blown flood that can wash away whole villages and hillsides. And there's nothing you can do to stop it.

Pretty grim, isn't it? But is it all doom and gloom? Or can the rot really be stopped? Time to find out what's being done to save the bloomin' rainforests…

A BLOOMIN FUTURE!

Unless something's done to save them soon, there won't be any rainforests left. The good news is that conservation groups, governments and local people all over the world are working hard to stop the rot. But saving the rainforest isn't as straightforward as it sounds. Many rainforests grow in poor, overcrowded countries. Thousands of people from chockful cities are forced into the forests to find enough space to live. And rich countries pay them lots of much-needed dosh for timber and other rainforest treasures. It's a horribly tricky business. Here are a few of the things people are trying to do:

1 National parks. These are protected patches of rainforest where logging and mining are banned. In the 1970s, the Kuna people of Panama set up their own reserve to save their traditional culture and the forest wildlife. Scientists or tourists must pay a fee to visit. No one else is allowed in. The Korup National Park in Cameroon, Africa, was set up in the 1980s. It is helping to protect hundreds of rare apes and monkeys and thousands of precious plants. Local people can hunt and fish in a ring of land around the park but not inside the park itself.

2 Planting trees. In many places, local people rely on the rainforests for firewood. They use the wood for cooking and heating. And it's putting the forest under great strain. Planting new trees can't replace the original forest (that takes thousands of years) but it certainly takes the pressure off it. In Brazil, scientists are busy bombing the forest with billions of tropical tree seeds to try to repair the damage. They fly over the forest and drop the seeds inside tiny balls of jelly to protect them as they land. Clever, eh?

3 Horrible holidays. For the holiday of a lifetime, why not check out the rainforest gorillas of Central Africa. They're some of the rarest animals on Earth. You'll need to save up – it's horribly costly – but you'll be doing your bit to keep the rainforests in one piece. Some of your hard-earned cash helps protect the apes' forest home. Some helps the local people. But be warned. You'll be made very welcome, but only as long as you don't leave any litter and you treat the rainforest with respect.

4 Rainforest perfumes. People are looking at ways of using rainforest resources without ruining the forest. Want to do your bit to save the rainforests? And do your Christmas shopping at the same time? Why not treat your mum to a nice big bottle of the gorgeous, the lovely, the delectable … Essence of Rainforest?

ESSENCE of

RAINFOREST

The fabulous forest fragrance that will really get right up your nose!

TAKE YOUR PICK FROM OUR BRAND NEW RANGE OF Sensational Forest Scents

OUR GUARANTEE TO YOU

THESE PUNGENT PONGS ARE COLLECTED BY US FROM EXCLUSIVE RAINFOREST BLOOMERS. FLOWERS NO ONE HAS EVER SMELLED BEFORE. THAT'S HOW BLOOMIN' RARE THEY ARE. BUT DON'T WORRY - THE RAINFOREST'S SAFE IN OUR HANDS. WE DON'T EVEN HAVE TO PICK THEM. USING THE LATEST TECHNOLOGY, WE SEAL EACH FLOWER IN A GLASS GLOBE, THEN DUMP ALL THE AIR OUT. INCLUDING THE SMELL.
WITHOUT HARMING A SINGLE PETAL.

122

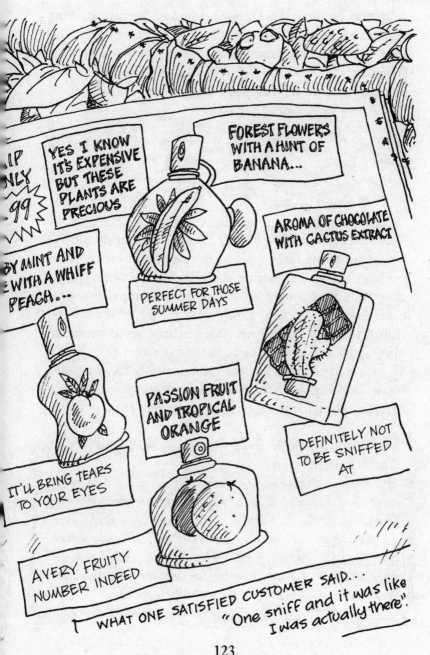

123

5 Iguana farming. That's right, iguanas. Iguanas are long lizards that normally lounge about in rainforest trees. But they also make ideal farm animals.

When German geographer Dr Dagmar Werner decided to set up an iguana farm, people thought she was crazy. Why couldn't she stick to boring sheep and cows like everybody else? Well, local people like eating iguana. (Apparently they taste a bit like chicken. Fancy a tasty plate of iguana and chips?) But so much rainforest has been chopped down and so many iguanas hunted, they're becoming rather rare. So Dr Werner rears them on her farm, then releases them into the forest. That way, people have enough to eat and are encouraged to protect the iguanas' tree homes. Ingenious, eh?

Earth-shattering fact
If there isn't a rainforest near where you live, why not grow your own indoors? That's what scientists are doing in Cornwall, England. They've built an enormous greenhouse (as big as four soccer pitches and 60 metres tall) and planted more than 10,000 rare rainforest plants inside, including some huge rubber trees. Visitors can ride around the rainforest on a small train. Why not pop along and take a peak?

A bloomin' future?

The burning question is: will any of these campaigns really work? Or are scientists fighting a losing battle? The truth is, nobody knows for certain. And unfortunately time's running out. Fast! Left alone, bloomin' rainforests might grow back but it'll take thousands of years. And they'll never be quite the same again. Scientists agree that one way to persuade people to save the forests is to teach them how vital and valuable they are. Before it's too bloomin' late. So why not grab a victim ... I mean, friend ... and bamboozle them with your new-found forest knowledge? Better still, start with your very own geography teacher. Unless she's sneaked back to Planet Blob, of course.

HORRIBLE INDEX

IT'S A
JUNGLE IN
THERE

HORRIBLE GEOGRAPHY

BLOOMIN'
RAINFORESTS

ANITA GANERI ILLUSTRATED BY MIKE PHILLIPS

SCHOLASTIC

Also available
Cracking Coasts · Desperate Deserts · Earth-Shattering Earthquakes
Freaky Peaks · Monster Lakes · Odious Oceans · Perishing Poles
Raging Rivers · Stormy Weather · Violent Volcanoes · Wild Islands

Horrible Geography Handbooks
Planet in Peril
Wicked Weather
Wild Animals

Specials
Intrepid Explorers
Horrible Geography of the World

Scholastic Children's Books,
Euston House, 24 Eversholt Street,
London, NW1 1DB, UK

A division of Scholastic Ltd
London ~ New York ~ Toronto ~ Sydney ~ Auckland
Mexico City ~ New Delhi ~ Hong Kong

First published in the UK by Scholastic Ltd, 2001
This edition published by Scholastic Ltd, 2008

Text copyright © Anita Ganeri, 2001
Illustrations copyright © Mike Phillips, 2001, 2008

ISBN 978 0439 94460 1

All rights reserved

Printed and bound by CPI Group (UK) Ltd, Croydon, CR0 4YY

22

The right of Anita Ganeri and Mike Phillips to be identified as the author and illustrator of this work
respectively has been asserted by them in accordance with the Copyright, Designs and
Patents Act, 1988.

Papers used by Scholastic Children's Books are made from woods grown in sustainable forests.

Título original: *La sombra del cazador*

Primera edición: marzo de 2012

©Texto: Álvaro Magalhães
©Ilustraciones: Carlos J. Campos
©Edición original: Edições ASA II, S.A., Portugal, 2010

© de la traducción: Juanjo Berdullas
© de esta edición: Libros del Atril S.L.,
Av. Marquès de l'Argentera, 17, Pral.
08003 Barcelona
www.piruetaeditorial.com

Impreso por Liberduplex, s.l.u.
ISBN: 978-84-15235-25-5
Depósito legal: B- 5134-2012

Álvaro Magalhães

Crónicas del Vampiro Valentín

Libro 5

La sombra del cazador

Ilustraciones de Carlos J. Campos

pirueta

El abuelo

El padre

La madre

Valentín

Dientecilla

Milhombres

SINF
SINF

Madroño

LA MUCHACHA MISTERIOSA

En casa, Adolfo Milhombres miraba entristecido el retrato del que su padre seguía ausente.

NECESITAMOS UN PLAN
PARA ATRAPAR AL GATO O NO VOLVERÁ,
Y ESTE VACÍO ES

¡INSOPORTABLE!

¿Y SI HACEMOS CHORIZOS QUE
NOS SIRVAN DE CEBO?

NI HABLAR. NO SOPORTO EL OLOR.
ME DAN NÁUSEAS SOLO DE OÍRLO. NECESITAMOS
UN PLAN SIN CEBOS NI CHORIZOS.

ENTONCES ES FÁCIL. VAMOS ALLÍ Y
¡ZAS!
EL PLAN ES SIEMPRE ASÍ.

—Esta vez, tenemos que pensar algo; no podemos llegar y **¡ZAS!**. Tiene que ser algo distinto —dijo Milhombres.

El ayudante se rascó la cabeza.

¿Y SI LLEGAMOS Y

ZAS CATAPLÁS?

NO ME DIRÁ QUE NO ES ALGO DISTINTO.

Madroño se rio mucho, algo extraño en un hombre tan gris y aburrido.

Tuvo suerte de que Milhombres estuviera demasiado ocupado pensando en un plan sin cebos ni chorizos.

SE VENDE
22 4437122

Se inclinó sobre la fotografía de
la fachada de los Perestrelo, que estaba
sobre la mesa, y reparó en que la casa de al lado
estaba en venta.

—Eso es. La casa de al lado... —dijo entonces—.
Esa casa será nuestro **CUARTEL GENERAL**.
Si estamos allí mismo, no nos harán falta planos.
Podemos ir por el jardín y entrar por detrás, pasar
por el tejado y hacer un agujero en el sótano.

¿Ve usted mi cabeza? No para de maquinar. ¡Para, cabeza!

La cabeza dejó de maquinar.

—¿Ya tenemos operación? —preguntó Madroño, confuso.

Milhombres respondió:

OPERACIÓN CUARTEL GENERAL

—¿Qué tal? Y, ahora, disfracémonos.

¿DISFRAZARNOS? ¿DE QUÉ? NO ESTAMOS EN CARNAVAL.

PRONTO LO VERÁ. ES CARNAVAL SIEMPR[E] QUE HACE FALTA.

A esa hora, cerca de las nueve de la noche, Valentín llegaba a casa. Estaba destrozado por haber perdido a Diana y no saber cómo buscarla. Tenía los ojos **hinchados** y **rojos** de llorar; el corazón le latía débilmente en alguna parte del pecho. ¿Para qué lo quería?

Fue directo a su cuarto, sin hablar con nadie, pero Dientecilla lo siguió y llamó a la puerta.

VALENTÍN, NO PUEDES IMAGINARTE LO QUE HA OCURRIDO...

—He descubierto que Piñero es nuestro bisabuelo. O mejor dicho, que era nuestro bisabuelo. ¡El alma, la lucecilla blanca, es él!

—¿CÓMO DICES? —preguntó Valentín, confuso, abriendo la puerta.

Su hermana entró, al instante, y le explicó:

FUIMOS AL CEMENTERIO Y LA FOTOGRAFÍA DE NUESTRO BISABUELO ERA IGUAL QUE EL RETRATO DE PIÑERO QUE ENCONTRÉ EN EL SÓTANO. ¿QUIERES VERLO?

NO, YA HE TENIDO MI PROPIA DOSIS. VENGO TAMBIÉN DEL CEMENTERIO...

Y ÉL TAMBIÉN ERA UN VAMPIRO NADA CORRIENTE, COMO NOSOTROS.

—  ¿Piñero?  ¿Bisabuelo? ¿Era como nosotros? —preguntó Valentín, más interesado.

—Sí, solo que acabó muriendo y ahora es aquella lucecilla que nos trajo hasta aquí y nos dio la casa y los nuevos nombres. Desde que descubrimos de quién era el alma, no la hemos vuelto a ver. Ha sido una ventolera que le ha dado.

SON DEMASIADAS COSAS.

¿Y TÚ? ¿FUE MAL LA CITA CON LA MUCHACHA? ¿LE DIJISTE QUIÉN ERAS Y HUYÓ?

—No. Desapareció. No llegamos
ni a darnos nuestros números,
las direcciones, nada...

—¿Qué hicisteis entonces? —quiso saber Dientecilla.

—Nada —respondió su hermano—. Hablamos,
paseamos, miramos las estrellas. ¿Sabías que vivimos
en la Tierra y en el Cielo? Yo tampoco. Ahora lo sé.
Y también sé quién es ella.

OTRA COMO NOSOTROS.

Incluso fui a su tumba. Murió hace cinco años,
imagínate.

¿OTRA COMO NOSOTROS?
¿HAS ENCONTRADO A OTRA
COMO NOSOTROS? ¡ES INCREÍBLE,
HOMBRE! TU NOTICIA ES MÁS
IMPORTANTE QUE LA MÍA.

Y, dicho esto, Dientecilla
abrió la puerta y gritó:

¡VALENTÍN HA ENCONTRADO
A OTRA COMO NOSOTROS!

El abuelo y la madre se
acercaron corriendo.
El abuelo, porque

«OTROS COMO NOSOTROS»

era su asunto preferido; la madre,
porque quería saber en que lío
se había metido Valentín.

¿QUIÉN ES?
¿DÓNDE ESTÁ ESE OTRO QUE ES
COMO NOSOTROS?

El abuelo entró en el cuarto
de repente.

¡NO ES OTRO, ES OTRA!

Valentín, de muy mal
humor, casi gritó a su abuelo.
Luego, salió de su habitación.

Los demás lo siguieron escaleras abajo hasta el salón, donde su padre seguía inclinado sobre el calendario lunar, completamente ajeno a todo lo demás.

—Escuchad esto —dijo—. El bisabuelo Perestrelo, quiero decir, el padre del abuelo, murió un 25 de junio, como nosotros. Reparé en eso en el cementerio y he estado pensando si era algo más que una mera coincidencia.

—Un momento —dijo Valentín, súbitamente interesado—. Ella también murió un 25 de junio.

—¿Quién es ella? —preguntó su padre.

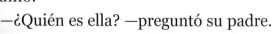

LA MUCHACHA QUE ES COMO NOSOTROS.

—Valentín la conoció y luego descubrió que había muerto... —añadió Dientecilla.

Valentín se acercó a su padre y a los dos calendarios que había sobre la mesa y lo confirmó:

UN 25 DE JUNIO.

YA SOMOS MUCHOS: EL BISABUELO, NOSOTROS Y LA MUCHACHA QUE VALENTÍN CONOCIÓ. PERO ¿QUIÉN ERA?

Valentín les mostró el recorte de periódico que guardaba cuidadosamente en el bolsillo de la camisa, junto al pecho.

Diana Rodrigues de Melo
Fallecida el 25 de junio de 2005

NO ERA DE AQUÍ. SOLO QUERÍA VER EL MAR Y EL CIELO. DECÍA: «VIVIMOS EN LA TIERRA Y EN EL CIELO». CONOCÍA LOS NOMBRES DE LAS ESTRELLAS Y SE FIJABA EN LOS BICHOS DE LA TIERRA, SOBRE TODO EN LOS MÁS PEQUEÑOS.

—Es una muchacha encantadora —dijo el abuelo.

—Es verdad —coincidió Valentín—. ¡Díselo a mi corazón!

—¡El amor hace daño, Valentín! —dijo la madre.

—Pues sí, es verdad.

Y el abuelo:

—Ah, **el Amor**... Es verdad que puede ser un sufrimiento, pero quien no lo conoce está bien muerto.

—**¡ES MI CASO!**

—gritó Dientecilla, y añadió emocionada:

NINGÚN CHICO SE ENAMORARÁ DE MÍ ASÍ... **¡QUiERO CRECER!**

Hacía tiempo que no decía que quería crecer y todas esas cosas, pero, en esta situación, no podía evitarlo. No se podía hacer nada: solo esperar que acabara y consolarla. Lo de costumbre.

EL DÍA FUERA DEL TIEMPO

Cuando al fin Dientecilla se calmó, volvieron al mismo tema:

La Misteriosa Diana.

Rodrigues de ... da el 25 de junio de 2005

...lebrará mañana ...en el cementerio ...reposará ...nteón familiar.

—Creo que no vive aquí —dijo Valentín.

—¿Y entonces? ¿Dónde vive? —preguntó el padre sin levantar la vista de los calendarios que estaba estudiando.

—En el **Mundo de Allá** —respondió Valentín—. ¿Ya os habéis olvidado del Mundo de Allá? Allí es donde viven los que son como nosotros. Al menos la mayor parte de ellos. Y algunos deben andar de acá para allá, como ella.

Los demás rodearon a Valentín, atentos. Querían saber más sobre la misteriosa muchacha del Mundo de Allá. Parecían niños a la espera de escuchar un cuento.

Valentín fue a buscar la cartera de Diana y esparció las cosas que había dentro sobre la mesa.

—Todas estas cosas son del Mundo de Allá —dijo
él—. Una crema de día
de una marca que
no existe; una
tarjeta de crédito
de un banco
que tampoco
existe; y una
entrada para un concierto
de Michael Jackson en el Centro
Pipistrello, que tampoco existe.

—Ni tampoco existe
Michael Jackson.
Murió, ya no está AQUÍ...

—Por eso mismo. Tal vez ahora, esté ALLÁ.

El abuelo se rascó la cabeza:

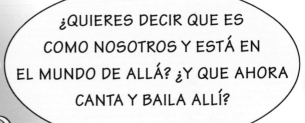

¿QUIERES DECIR QUE ES
COMO NOSOTROS Y ESTÁ EN
EL MUNDO DE ALLÁ? ¿Y QUE AHORA
CANTA Y BAILA ALLÍ?

—¿Y también murió **un 25 de junio**? —preguntó el padre—. Fue el verano pasado, pero el día...

—Lo miraron en Internet y allí estaba: Michael Jackson había muerto el 25 de junio de 2009.

El padre recapituló, con la excitación de quien está a punto de hacer un **GRAN DESCUBRIMIENTO:**

NOSOTROS, EL BISABUELO, LA MUCHACHA MISTERIOSA, MICHAEL JACKSON... YA SOMOS OCHO LOS QUE MORIMOS EL 25 DE JUNIO Y AÚN ANDAMOS POR AQUÍ. CREO QUE HEMOS DESCIFRADO NUESTRO SECRETO.

¿QUIERES DECIR QUE SOMOS ASÍ PORQUE MORIMOS **EL 25 DE JUNIO**?

Allí estaba

EL GRAN DESCUBRIMIENTO

Pero ¿qué rayos ocurría el día 25 de junio?

—Es el día fuera del tiempo —explicó el padre—. En el calendario lunar, el 25 de junio es el día fuera del tiempo.

—Si está fuera del tiempo, tendrá que ver con nosotros —dijo Dientecilla, interesada.

¿Y a quién podía no interesarle esa novedad? Esta vez, todos rodearon al padre, como niños ávidos de una buena historia, y él levantó la vista hacia el techo de la sala, como si allí estuviera el cielo. Después dijo:

—¡Escuchen con atención, que esto no es una lección! La Tierra tarda 365 días en dar la vuelta alrededor del Sol. ¿Cierto?

—Cierto.

—La Luna tarda 52 semanas y 7 días en completar sus cuatro ciclos, lo que suma 364 días. Por lo tanto, a la Luna le sobra un día. ¿Cierto? Ese día es el 25 de junio, que no participa del ciclo lunar. Es el día fuera del tiempo, un día en que el mundo para y recupera el aliento. ¿Estoy o no en lo cierto?

¡GRAN DESCUBRIMIENTO!

Ahora sabían por qué se habían despertado del sueño de la Muerte.

SI HUBIÉRAMOS MUERTO UN DÍA ANTES O DESPUÉS, NO ESTARÍAMOS AQUÍ EXPERIMENTANDO NUEVAS FORMAS DE ANDAR POR LA VIDA.

EN ESE CASO, BASTA CON BUSCAR EN EL PERIÓDICO A LOS QUE MURIERON UN **25 DE JUNIO**. SERÁN COMO NOSOTROS. HABRÁ MUCHOS. SOLO AQUÍ, MUEREN DECENAS DE PERSONAS TODOS LOS DÍAS. IMAGÍNATE EN EL MUNDO ENTERO.

—Calma. Aún no lo sabemos todo. Además de eso, muchos, la mayoría, acaban encerrados en ataúdes bajo tierra. No consiguen salir y acaban por morir del todo allí mismo. Y también mueren los incinerados. Nosotros tuvimos la suerte de ir a parar a un panteón familiar.

IMAGÍNATE SI NO HUBIÉRAMOS TENIDO PANTEÓN FAMILIAR...

Ya era el segundo **«SI»** (si no hubiéramos muerto un 25 de junio, si no hubiéramos tenido panteón familiar). Pero había más. La vida está hecha de **«SÍES»**, de muchos **«SÍES»**.

—¿Y **Si** comemos algo? —preguntó el abuelo—. Esta conversación me ha dado hambre.

—Aun así, debe haber miles, millones como nosotros en el mundo entero —reflexionó el padre.

—Pero ¿dónde están para que no los veamos?

— **ESCONDIDOS**, como nosotros —dijo Dientecilla.

—En el Mundo de Allá —dijo Valentín—. Allá es donde están. Pero la cuestión es: ¿cómo se va al Mundo de Allá?

¡AY, QUÉ ALIVIO! AUNQUE NO LOS CONOZCAMOS, ES BUENO SABER QUE ESTAMOS ACOMPAÑADOS, QUE NO ESTAMOS SOLOS.

Mundo de Allá,
Mundo de Allá.

Cada vez llegaban más noticias del Mundo de Allá, cada vez estaban más cerca del Mundo de Allá. Solo les faltaba llegar a él.

Entretanto, en casa de Adolfo Milhombres,
el viejo cazador y su ayudante acababan de
ENSUCIARSE Y TIZNARSE, después de haber
rasgado la ropa más vieja que habían encontrado. Al
final, se miraron al espejo y se vieron como dos
verdaderos sin techo. Ese era el disfraz.

—¿Qué dirá mi mujer...? —se quejó Madroño.

> CÁLLESE YA CON SU MUJER. Y MUÉVASE. TENEMOS QUE ATRAPAR AL MALDITO GATO O MI PADRE NO VOLVERÁ. Y DÍGAME: ¿CON QUIÉN HABLARÉ ENTONCES? NO TENGO A NADIE MÁS.

Madroño no respondió,
pero pensó:

> TIENE A GLORIA. BIEN QUE PODRÍA CASARSE CON ELLA.

—¿Qué está pensando? —preguntó
Milhombres, desconfiado.

—¿Yo? Nada —respondió Madroño sonrojado.

«El pensamiento es libre
—pensó—, ¿o no?»

> JURARÍA QUE ESTABA PENSANDO QUE YO Y...

Antes de que pudiera pronunciar la palabra, llamaron a la puerta y era Gloria, la vecina de abajo que lo perseguía para pintarlo (y vaya usted a saber para qué más).

—¿Está disponible, profesor? —preguntó desde el otro lado de la puerta.

—Caramba, no he llegado a decir **«GLORIA»** y aun así ha aparecido... —se lamentó Milhombres mientras empujaba a Madroño.

—Deprisa, hombre. Bajemos por la escalera de servicio, por la parte de atrás. Estas mujeres que no tienen nada que hacer se creen que la vida es un juego.

CAPÍTULO III
LA SOMBRA DEL CAZADOR

Milhombres y su ayudante, disfrazados de sin techo, bajaron a la calle. No habían dado ni siquiera diez pasos cuando una señora le dio una limosna a Madroño.

Él le devolvió la moneda, amablemente.

—Gracias, pero esto no es más que un disfraz —dijo.

—¿Un disfraz? —preguntó la señora—. Aún cree que es poco, ¿no? Mira tú, un pobre que encima responde mal.

Milhombres empujó a Madroño, casi levantándolo en el aire, mientras le susurraba al oído:

TIENE QUE ACEPTAR LAS LIMOSNAS. ESO FORMA PARTE TAMBIÉN DEL DISFRAZ. SI NO LAS ACEPTA, LA GENTE SE DARÁ CUENTA ENSEGUIDA DE QUE NO ES UN SIN TECHO.

¡AH!

Como si fuera a propósito, para probarlo, poco después le dieron otra limosna. La aceptó y se la guardó en el desharrapado bolsillo.

—¿Lo ve? —dijo Milhombres—. No cuesta nada. Ah, el disfraz da el pego, es perfecto, es perfecto.

Milhombres estaba animado, pero no paraba de mirar hacia atrás, desconfiado. Tenía la impresión de que alguien los seguía (y tenía razón, el Hombre Misterioso que los espiaba andaba por allí).

—Es solo una impresión —consideró Madroño, mientras agradecía una nueva limosna—. ¿Quién podría seguirnos?

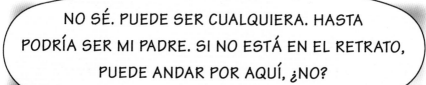

NO SÉ. PUEDE SER CUALQUIERA. HASTA PODRÍA SER MI PADRE. SI NO ESTÁ EN EL RETRATO, PUEDE ANDAR POR AQUÍ, ¿NO?

¿NO ESTABA MUERTO?

SI, MURIÓ, PERO LA MUERTE NO ES EL FINAL. ¿AÚN NO HA APRENDIDO NADA? ¿NO VE LOS VAMPIROS QUE PERSIGO? MURIERON, PERO AÚN SIGUEN AQUÍ.

¿EL PADRE DEL PROFESOR TAMBIÉN ES UN VAMPIRO?

—No, hombre. No solo
hay vampiros: hay almas,
espíritus. Todo eso existe.
Y el alma de mi padre aún
anda por aquí. ¿Sabe por qué?
Porque murió sin cumplir su
mayor tarea. Cuando se muere, no se
puede dejar nada importante por hacer.
O entonces hay un problema.
El alma no consigue elevarse y se queda
rondando para ver si se resuelven
las cosas.

Madroño se estremeció y dijo:

—No me asuste, profesor.

Por fin habían llegado
a la Avenida de los
Combatientes, donde
estaba la casa de los
Perestrelo, y Madroño
recibió dos nuevas
limosnas a la entrada
de la estación de metro.

LLEVO CASI VEINTE EUROS Y NO HEMOS HECHO MÁS QUE COMENZAR. PUEDE QUE CAMBIE DE PROFESIÓN…

Entretanto, en casa de los Perestrelo, el abuelo se fue a su cuarto a descansar. Estaba abrumado con la avalancha de misterios y novedades de las últimas horas. Ya no tenía edad para tantas emociones. El padre salió y fue a investigar a los archivos de los periódicos; quería hacer una lista de las personas que habían muerto un **25 de junio** en los últimos años.

37

Dientecilla intentó que su hermano se interesara por el **MISTERIO DEL ALMACÉN** donde Celeste desaparecía, pero él no estaba para esas cosas. Ya tenía suficiente con el misterio de Diana y del Mundo de Allá. Quería estar al aire libre, bajo la luz de las estrellas; y tal vez volver a la cafetería de la playa, donde había dejado aviso por si Diana aparecía buscando la cartera.

—Los misterios, de uno en uno —dijo antes de salir.

Dientecilla se fue al cuarto
a ver la televisión y abrió
la ventana que daba a la calle.
Y entonces vio, en el paseo,
la sombra, también gorda,
del cazador de vampiros.
Si su sombra estaba allí,
el cazador no podía andar
lejos. No hay hombre sin
sombra. Un hombre es él
y su sombra.

Cerró la ventana, saltó a la cama y se tapó la
cabeza con la manta. Y allí se quedó durante un rato,
escuchando y con los ojos
bien abiertos. Y, entonces,
oyó pasos en el pasillo.
Con un hilo de voz dijo:

¡MAMÁ! ¡ABUELO!

39

Se levantó para escapar de allí, pero los pasos cada vez sonaban más próximos. Ya no tenía tiempo. Tampoco conseguiría huir aunque quisiera; estaba paralizada y era incapaz de mover un dedo. Fuera quien fuera, estaba allí, detrás de aquella puerta. Dientecilla intentó gritar para llamar a su madre, que estaba en el piso de abajo, y tampoco lo consiguió. Las palabras tenían miedo de salir y se escondían dentro de ella, en algún lugar oscuro.

El picaporte giró, la puerta chirrió y se entreabrió. La luz débil del corredor proyectó la sombra del intruso en la pared del fondo del cuarto. Dientecilla vio crecer en la pared la sombra del cazador, con una estaca de madera en la mano derecha.

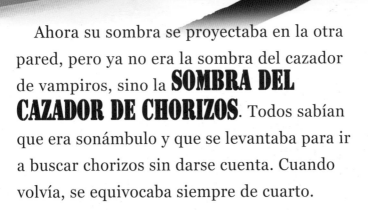

Dientecilla soltó un grito agudo que no llegó a salir. En alguna parte de su garganta había un nudo que no dejaba pasar nada; pero fue capaz de extender el brazo para encender la luz y entonces vio que, en la puerta del cuarto, estaba el abuelo, con un chorizo en la mano.

Ahora su sombra se proyectaba en la otra pared, pero ya no era la sombra del cazador de vampiros, sino la **SOMBRA DEL CAZADOR DE CHORIZOS**. Todos sabían que era sonámbulo y que se levantaba para ir a buscar chorizos sin darse cuenta. Cuando volvía, se equivocaba siempre de cuarto.

Como dicen que no
se debe despertar a
los sonámbulos, Dientecilla
empujó al abuelo
delicadamente hasta
su cuarto; y como
el aroma del chorizo
le abrió el apetito, fue
a la cocina a buscar
las sobras del desayuno.

En mitad de las escaleras, vio que Celeste salía
de la cocina con una bandeja de chorizos en la mano
en dirección al sótano. Se agachó para que no la
viera y después la siguió, en calcetines. La detective
Dientecilla volvía a la acción.

Como la vez anterior, Dientecilla vio a Celeste
entrar en el almacén. Fue a mirar por la cerradura
y ya no estaba. Ese era el misterio: Celeste entraba
allí y desaparecía. Como el alma, se marchaba sin
haberse ido.

Sentada en un viejo arcón de madera, Dientecilla
esperó a que Celeste apareciera, si es que iba a
hacerlo. Ya se sabía: en aquella casa, todo podía
pasar. Media hora después no había pasado nada.
¿Se había marchado Celeste para siempre, a otra
casa distinta, a otro mundo, a otra dimensión?

No. La puerta del almacén se movió y allí estaba Celeste de nuevo.

— ¡UY, QUÉ SUSTO! —dijo cuando vio a Dientecilla.

La bandeja, ahora vacía, fue a parar al suelo.

—¿Quién se ha comido todos esos chorizos? —preguntó Dientecilla—. ¿Y cómo desapareces apenas entras en el almacén?

Celeste, sonrojada, estaba confusa, nerviosa, y volvió a dejar caer la bandeja.

UY, PEQUEÑA, NO QUIERAS SABERLO. Y NUNCA ENTRES EN EL ALMACÉN. TAMBIÉN PODRÍAS DESAPARECER.

CAPÍTULO IV
LA HISTORIA DEL HOMBRE-RATA

Fueron al salón y de allí pasaron a la cocina, donde Celeste limpió la bandeja. Miró a Dientecilla y vio que esperaba una explicación. Entonces dijo:
—Sabes, pequeña, un día estaba aquí sacando unos chorizos del horno y vi que detrás había un hombre horroroso, cubierto de pelo y con la nariz afilada. Era el Hombre-Rata.

Ya había oído hablar de él, pero pensaba que sólo era una leyenda. Cuentan que lo abandonaron de pequeño en las alcantarillas y que sobrevivió comiendo ratas. Comió tantas que acabó pareciéndose a ellas. Somos lo que comemos, ¿no lo has oído nunca?

Dientecilla se puso a imaginar al Hombre-Rata, y también cómo sería *un Hombre-Lagarto, un Hombre-Sapo, un Hombre-Tiburón. Y una Niña-Iguana, una Mujer-Sardina...*

Celeste interrumpió las imaginaciones de Dientecilla.

—Y allí estaba —continuó—. Estoy segura de que iba a comerme. Era lo que decían sus ojos, su mirada hambrienta. Pero le llegó al hocico (sí, tenía hocico) el olor de los chorizos recién salidos del horno y, sin poder resistirse, se los comió todos. Cuando acabó, dijo: «A partir de hoy, llevarás una bandeja de chorizos al almacén del sótano o mandaré una plaga de ratas para que os coman durante la noche». Y por eso todas las noches llevo un plato de chorizos al Hombre-Rata.

Llamaron a la puerta. Celeste fue a abrir y era el señor Lobo, el fontanero, y su ayudante, el señor Cordero. Venían a arreglar los grifos de la cocina. Un lobo y un cordero. Y congeniaban, eran un equipo. «Si se transformaran en su nombre, iba a ser bonito», pensó Dientecilla.

Muchas personas tienen nombres de animales. El señor y la señora Carnero, Pardal, León, Palomo, Becerra, Buey, Toro, Pato, Conejo, Zorrilla y otros. Y no es tan raro, porque, aunque a veces lo olviden, las personas también son animales.

BUENO, VOY ARRIBA A ARREGLAR LOS CUARTOS. ¡TENGO TANTO QUE HACER!

¿Y CÓMO ATRAVIESAS LA PARED DEL ALMACÉN?

Dientecilla la acompañó. Aquello no podía quedar así.

Celeste suspiró profundamente.

Después respondió:

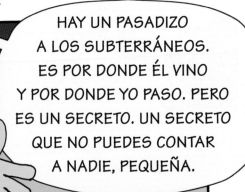

HAY UN PASADIZO A LOS SUBTERRÁNEOS. ES POR DONDE ÉL VINO Y POR DONDE YO PASO. PERO ES UN SECRETO. UN SECRETO QUE NO PUEDES CONTAR A NADIE, PEQUEÑA.

VALE, VALE, ES UNA BUENA HISTORIA. ME ENCANTAN LAS HISTORIAS, INCLUSO LAS HORRIPILANTES COMO ESA. PERO AHORA ME GUSTARÍA QUE ME DIJERAS LA VERDAD, AUNQUE SEA MENOS INTERESANTE.

¡AH, LA VERDAD! LA VERDAD ES QUE NO EXISTE NINGÚN HOMBRE-RATA. ESO ERA LO QUE ME DECÍA MI MADRE PARA QUE ME COMIERA LA SOPA. AÚN HOY ME LA COMO POR ESO. PERO ESTÁ EL ALMA DEL SEÑOR PIÑERO. LE GUSTAN LOS CHORIZOS HASTA HARTARSE. TODOS LOS DÍAS SE COME DOS O TRES.

Dientecilla lanzó a Celeste una mirada de advertencia. Como si le dijera: no me vuelvas a mentir.

ES VERDAD, ESA ES LA VERDAD.
YO TAMPOCO LO CREÍA, PERO
AHORA SÉ QUE LAS ALMAS
TAMBIÉN SE ALIMENTAN.
Y DE CHORIZOS DE ESOS...

Dientecilla, la detective
Dientecilla, arrugó la nariz.

¡PERO YO TE
ESTABA ESPIANDO!
NO ESTABAS ALLÍ.
DESAPARECISTE.

—Esa es la clave
—respondió Celeste.
—La lucecilla me
lanza un polvo por
encima que me da
el poder de atravesar
la pared.

Al otro lado hay otra sala, donde vive el alma.
Pongo los chorizos encima de una mesita y espero.
Ella da vueltas alrededor de los chorizos; parece que
solo los huele y los mira, pero lo cierto es que acaban
desapareciendo.

Dientecilla no entendía mucho de almas, hasta
hace poco no sabía que existieran; y también prefería
que aquello fuera obra de un alma y no de un
horroroso Hombre-Rata.

Pero aun así desconfiaba. Sabía que al menos
la mitad de aquella historia era un invento.

—Esa es la verdad —concluyó Celeste—. No se lo cuentes a nadie. ¿Me lo prometes?

Dientecilla cruzó los dedos detrás de la espalda, mientras, muy seria, decía:

—¡Lo prometo!

Mientras, allí al lado, Milhombres y Madroño se preparaban para entrar en la casa deshabitada. La Operación Cuartel General estaba en marcha.

Fue entonces cuando, por la ventana por la que iban a entrar, salió un verdadero sin techo.

Llevaba una maleta vieja y parecía horrorizado, con los cabellos encrespados y erizados.

YO EN VUESTRO LUGAR NO ENTRARÍA EN ESTA CASA. AHÍ DENTRO OCURREN COSAS EXTRAÑAS. TAMBIÉN ERA RARO, ¿NO?, UNA CASA TAN GRANDE Y EN TAN BUEN ESTADO Y SIN NADIE DENTRO. NO PODÍA SER. VENGO DE UNA CASA PEQUEÑA EN LA QUE VIVEN MÁS DE VEINTE OCUPAS.

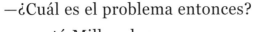

—¿Cuál es el problema entonces?
—preguntó Milhombres.

—El espíritu, o el fantasma,
o lo que sea, de la mujer
que vivía aquí, una actriz
—respondió el sin techo.

—¿Quién era?
—preguntó Madroño, y
Milhombres le dio una
palmada en la espalda para que se callara.

Había una placa de metal, al lado de la puerta,
con la siguiente inscripción:

**Aquí nació,
vivió y murió
la gran actriz
de teatro
Palmira Zambullida
(1925-1987).**

El sin techo se marchó refunfuñando.

—¿Ha oído eso, profesor? —preguntó Madroño.

—Tengo buen oído, ¿no lo sabe usted? —gritó Milhombres—. No son más que tretas. A mí con fantasmas. Un cazador de vampiros no teme a esas cosas...

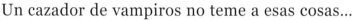

¿QUÉ COSAS?

ALMAS, ESPÍRITUS... COSAS QUE EXISTEN, PERO QUE NO PODEMOS VER, SOLO SENTIMOS QUE EXISTEN. AHORA DÍGAME UNA...

—¿Una qué?

—Una cosa que no se ve pero que existe.
Dígame una.

—A ver, a ver, quizá mi suegra —dijo Madroño—. No la veo desde la Pascua pasada.

—¿Qué suegra, ni suegra? Es el viento —aclaró Milhombres—. ¿Ha visto usted el viento?

Hacía un día espantoso, y Madroño miró la ventolera que los empujaba hacia atrás, pero no la vio.

—No se ve, el viento —reconoció entonces—. Solo lo sentimos, ¿no?

ESO ES: LOS ESPÍRITUS SON COMO EL VIENTO. SON OTRO TIPO DE VIENTO: LO PEOR QUE PUEDE PASAR ES QUE COJAMOS UN RESFRIADO. Y AHORA EN MARCHA. USTED DELANTE.

¿POR QUÉ? ¿NO SOY EL AYUDANTE?

LO ES, SÍ SEÑOR. POR ESO IRÁ DELANTE, PARA ABRIR CAMINO Y AYUDARME A PASAR.

CAPÍTULO V
LA CASA ENCANTADA

Entraron por la ventana por la que había salido el sin techo y avanzaron con pasos cortos y espaciados, con Madroño quejándose, en susurros, del aire helado.

También había cortinas viejas que se movían, sonidos que parecían gemidos de gente suspirando. Algo escalofriante.

—Parece como si me hablaran bajito al oído —gimió Madroño—. Y el aire cada vez es más helado. ¿No serán los espíritus? El profesor ha dicho que las almas son como el viento.

—¿Y qué? ¿Le hace algún mal?

—Me causa impresión, escalofríos; me tiembla todo.

Así, asustado y con todo el cuerpo temblándole, Madroño entró en el salón grande de la casa, que estaba completamente vacío. Solo había, en una pared, un retrato de una mujer baja y fuerte, de espesa cabellera y aire severo.

Era, claro está, la actriz Palmira Zambullida, la fallecida.

—Ay, Dios mío... —suspiró Madroño.

En ese momento, se oyó una voz, una voz de mujer, que aunque sonaba ronca, dijo:

¿Quién eres, tú que usurpas a estas horas de la noche el aire noble que ostentaba, el sepultado rey de Dinamarca?

—¿Qué significa eso? —dijo Madroño, horrorizado.

Temblaba tanto que le parecía que todo temblaba a su alrededor.

—Nada. No quiere decir nada. Es una obra de teatro —explicó Milhombres—. ¿No ve que la fallecida era actriz de teatro?

La voz gritó aún más alto:

¡Por los cielos, habla; te lo ordeno!

¿ES ELLA? ¿ES SU FANTASMA?

DEBE DE SERLO.

> ## ¡Salid de aquí, andrajosos apestosos!

—¿Eso también es teatro? —preguntó Madroño.

—No —respondió Milhombres—. Eso no.

—Entonces, será mejor que salgamos de aquí —dijo Madroño, reculando.

Milhombres lo empujó hacia delante.

—Avance, hombre. Abra aquella puerta.

> ## ¡Si sigues, caerás en el pozo del infierno!

Madroño volvió a recular.

—¿Eso también es teatro? —preguntó de nuevo.

—Sí que lo es —respondió Milhombres—. Avance.
O salga de ahí para que yo pueda entrar.

Milhombres avanzó y la voz se elevó, amenazante:

¡No des ni un solo paso más, gordo!

¿ESO TAMBIÉN ES TEATRO?

NO. ESO NO.

Milhombres
abrió la puerta
y siguió.

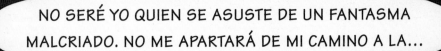

NO SERÉ YO QUIEN SE ASUSTE DE UN FANTASMA MALCRIADO. NO ME APARTARÁ DE MI CAMINO A LA...

¡PROFESOR!

Se tragó la palabra que iba a salir (¡Gloria, claro!) y se corrigió:

NO ME APARTARÁ DEL CAMINO DEL DEBER Y LA HONRA.

Fueron a parar al sótano, en el piso de abajo.
Cayeron sobre un montón de ropa. Tuvieron
suerte. Al lado mismo había una lavadora vieja y
las herramientas del jardín.

AAAAAHHHH

¿HEMOS CAÍDO AL POZO
DEL INFIERNO?

—Calle, hombre, esto es el sótano de la casa
—respondió Milhombres—. ¿Ve usted algún pozo
o algún infierno? Además, aquí era donde yo quería
llegar. El sótano de ellos está justo aquí al lado,
tal vez podamos hacer un agujero en la pared.
¿Qué le parece?

Se encendió una vela, en un rincón, y algo salió
de la oscuridad. ¿Qué sería?

Ser o no ser, esa es la cuestión.

Era una anciana, igualita a la del retrato del salón grande o, al menos, muy parecida. No andaba, se deslizaba, como si sus pies no tocaran el suelo. Y repitió:

Ser o no ser, esa es la cuestión.

—¿Eso también es teatro? —preguntó otra vez Madroño.

—¡Qué teatro, ni teatro! ¡Esto va en serio!

Pero Madroño ya no estaba para explicaciones. Pensó que, si empezaba a correr ya, podía ser el primero en salir.

Milhombres lo siguió escaleras arriba a gran velocidad y, en menos que canta un gallo, estaban saliendo de la casa encantada.

¡ADIÓS, DOÑA PALMIRA ZAMBULLIDA!

 ¡ARF! ¡ARF!

NOSOTROS SÍ QUE NOS HEMOS DADO UNA BUENA ZAMBULLIDA.

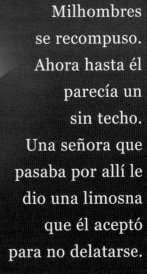

Milhombres se recompuso. Ahora hasta él parecía un sin techo. Una señora que pasaba por allí le dio una limosna que él aceptó para no delatarse.

¡AHORA SÍ QUE ESTÁ BIEN DISFRAZADO EL PROFESOR!

Madroño se rio de la escena. Pero no era el único que se reía. Dentro de la casa, en el último piso, el sin techo que había salido con la maleta para asustarlos (sí, aquello también era teatro) se reía abrazado a su mujer, que aún se estaba quitando las ropas antiguas.

TENDRÍAS QUE HABER VISTO LA CARA DEL GORDO CUANDO COMENCÉ A DESLIZARME SOBRE EL MONOPATÍN QUE LLEVABA DEBAJO DEL VESTIDO.

71

Milhombres, como veis, tenía razón: casi todo era teatro.

QUÉ BIEN QUE HAYAMOS DESPACHADO A ESTOS TAN DEPRISA. EMPIEZA LA TELENOVELA. ¡HACE FRÍO! ¿PREPARAS UN CAFÉ?

Vivían allí los dos, bien instalados en un cuarto con vistas a la calle, donde había todo tipo de objetos desperdigados: botellas vacías, bolsas de patatas fritas tiradas, un equipo de música y un televisor antiguo, una cama y dos sofás viejos.

Él volvió a mirar por la ventana.

—Ahí van esos dos. Pobres. Se han asustado de verdad. Me dan pena, pero así tiene que ser.

—Ah, esto sí que es vida —dijo ella. Y cantó, mientras ponía agua a calentar para el café:

SER POBRE Y SIN TECHO Y VIVIR EN CASA DE GENTE RICA SIN NADIE QUE TE MOLESTE, ¡ESO ES VIDA, ESO ES VIDA!

Él cerró la ventana y tambíen cantó:

A esa hora, Valentín vagueaba, desorientado,
por la ciudad. Pasó horas y horas en la puerta de la
Academia de Yoga. Para nada. Además, allí nadie
conocía a Diana, ni por el nombre, ni por la
descripción.

Ahora preguntaba a los árboles, al viento, a
las estrellas, a las piedras: «¿Dónde está el Mundo
de Allá? ¿Dónde queda? ¿Cómo se va al
Mundo de Allá?». Y nada. Entonces pensaba: «Daría
la vida por tener un número de teléfono,
una dirección». Pero nada. Ah, el Amor, quien
inventó el Amor no sabía lo que hacía.

—**¡Vaya palidez tan guay, tío!** —dijo una chica
vestida de negro que se puso a
caminar junto a él.

¿QUÉ?

ESAS OJERAS
TAMBIÉN MOLAN. ¿SON PINTADAS?
¿USAS ALGUNA CREMA?

—Es todo natural. No me pongo nada —respondió Valentín.

Ella le susurró al oído:

—¿También quieres ser gótico?

Él suspiró y dijo:

—Ya me gustaría ser algo. Fuera lo que fuera.

Ella no lo entendió e insistió:

—PÁSATE POR EL BAR PINGÜINO. ES UN BAR DE GÓTICOS.

—YO NO SOY GÓTICO —aclaró él.

¿ENTONCES, QUÉ ERES?

NO SOY NADA, NADIE. YA TE LO HE DICHO. NO EXISTO.

Y Valentín se alejó bruscamente. Se sentía cada vez más triste, más débil, casi a punto de desfallecer. (Pero ¡no estaba todo perdido, ya lo veréis!)

CAPÍTULO VI
HUYENDO DE GLORIA

Milhombres y Madroño regresaban a la base, mascando el fracaso.

—Otra operación fallida —dijo Madroño—. ¿Cómo se llamaba? Operación **Cuartel General**. Claro, si acababa en **«al»** tenía que ir mal. Debía haberse llamado, por ejemplo, Operación **Pastel de Belén**. Así seguro que habría acabado **bien**.

Iban tan maltrechos, tan abatidos, que la gente sentía pena y les daba más LIMOSNAS

—Al menos esta parte de la operación ha ido bien —comentó Madroño—. Le digo, profesor, que ganaría más como sin techo que como ayudante suyo.

—Cállese, hombre. Ser un sin techo no es una profesión, es no tener profesión alguna.

Siguieron andando, aunque con dificultades. Daban pena y la gente no paraba de darles limosna.

—Aún estoy pensando en aquello —dijo Milhombres deteniéndose—. No llegué a decir la palabra que no se puede decir; incluso dije por precaución: «No es de la Gloria», y aun así caí por el agujero del salón.

—Ahora la ha dicho —le recordó Madroño.

—**PUES SÍ...** —se lamentó Milhombres tapándose la boca.

Pero ya era tarde. Doblaron la esquina y ¿quién apareció? Pues, **GLORIA**, la vecina, la que quería hacerle un retrato (y quien sabe qué más).

Gloria le dio una limosna a Milhombres y se le quedó mirando, desconfiada:

SE PARECE MUCHO A UN CONOCIDO MÍO...

Milhombres no quería hablar para no delatarse y se limitó a encoger los hombros y a sonreír. Estaba pensando que solo le quedaba una opción: huir.
Por su parte, Gloria no se callaba. Quería saber cómo había llegado a tal miseria y esto y lo de más allá.
Peor aún: quería llevárselo a casa para darle sopa caliente, ropas de su marido fallecido, etc.

Y Milhombres, afligido, sudaba; no podía hablar, pero también le costaba estar callado (y Madroño, a su lado, se aguantaba la risa).

—ENTONCES, HASTA OTRA —dijo, por fin, cambiando la voz—. ACABO DE ACORDARME DE QUE TENGO COSAS QUE HACER.

¿NO ES UN SIN TECHO? LOS SIN TECHO NO TIENEN NADA QUE HACER.

QUIZÁ, PERO TENGO MUCHO QUE NO HACER. Y HOY AÚN NO HE NO HECHO NADA.

Dicho esto, Milhombres salió de allí apresuradamente (lo más rápido que podía, que era poco, claro está).

Aun así, corrió, con Madroño detrás, hasta perder el aliento, hasta que no supo dónde estaba. Solo dio con el camino a casa mucho después. Una vez allí, doloridos y cansados, pero ya libres de peligro, Milhombres y Madroño se sentaron en el sofá del salón y se durmieron uno junto al otro, como dos buenos sin techo.

Z Z Z Z Z Z Z Z Z Z Z Z

Más tarde, la mañana entró por la ventana del salón, pero despacio, para no despertarlos. Era un día gris (un día de esos), con mucho viento, y también entró por la ventana abierta una hoja de periódico voladora, que aterrizó en la nariz de Milhombres.

Se despertó y cogió la hoja.

—Es mi sección preferida, la de 𝕹𝖊𝖈𝖗𝖔𝖑𝖔́𝖌𝖎𝖈𝖆𝖘 —dijo—. Ha llegado volando.

Madroño también se despertó.

—¿Qué ha llegado volando?

—La página de 𝕹𝖊𝖈𝖗𝖔𝖑𝖔́𝖌𝖎𝖈𝖆𝖘 —respondió Milhombres—. Es la lista de los que han muerto y que van a enterrar hoy.

—Ah, pensé que había dicho 𝕹𝖊𝖈𝖗𝖔𝖑𝖔𝖌𝖎́𝖆, o algo parecido. ¿y todos han muerto de 𝕹𝖊𝖈𝖗𝖔𝖑𝖔𝖌𝖎́𝖆?

Milhombres ni lo oyó. Estaba con la boca abierta, mirando la página del periódico. De repente, dio un salto y se puso de pie.

—Aquí está: ha muerto otro Perestrelo —dijo—.
Eso es. Por eso el periódico ha venido a mí. Quizá ha
sido mi padre quien me lo ha mandado.

—Puede que lo haya traído él mismo —dijo
Madroño—. ¿Las almas no son un tipo de viento?

Milhombres miró el retrato donde
el padre seguía ausente.

¡GRACIAS, PAPÁ!
AHORA SÉ QUE NO ME
HAS ABANDONADO
DEL TODO.

Después, se volvió hacia Madroño y dio
sus órdenes:

—Vamos hacia el cementerio ahora mismo,
está a punto de empezar el entierro.

—¿Y cómo sabe que el muerto también es

Vampiro?

—quiso saber Madroño.

—Tiene que serlo, o no se llamaría Perestrelo —respondió Milhombres—. Lo llevan en la **Sangre**.

—Yo tuve un amigo Perestrelo y no era vampiro —insistió Madroño.

—¡Deje estar a su amigo! —gritó el viejo cazador, ya irritado—. ¿Su amigo era, acaso, de la familia de ellos?

—No lo sé —respondió Madroño.

—Perfecto —coincidió Madroño, muy contento—.
Todavía sacaré el dinero que me falta. En los
funerales siempre hay mucha gente.

A esa hora, en casa de los Perestrelo, el abuelo
estaba a mitad de la última comida de la noche,
ligerita, mientras leía el periódico que acababa de
llegar (también le gustaba empezar a leer el diario
por la página de necrológicas; también le gustaba
enterarse de quién había muerto).

—¡BASILIO! —dijo entonces—. BASILIO HA
MUERTO Y HOY ES EL ENTIERRO.

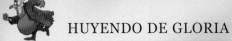

Miró por la ventana y vio que, en la calle, empezaba un día de aquellos en los que Valentín solía cantar: **¡MAÑANA CENICIENTA, SIN LUZ / ME HACE CANTAR, OLÉ OLÉ/ QUÉ BELLO DÍA HORRIBLE HACE HOY!** No era cuestión de cantar, al contrario; pero, en un día así, podía salir y asistir al entierro. Los demás estaban todos durmiendo y creyó que era mejor darles la noticia más tarde, cuando volviera. Luego se preparó para salir.

A la hora precisa, allí estaba, en el cementerio, pero a distancia, para que no le vieran.

Pensaba que estaba seguro, pero no. De repente, vio crecer a su lado la sombra del cazador de vampiros y se encogió del todo.

—¿Ha pasado por aquí un entierro? —preguntó, el sin techo Milhombres.

El abuelo señaló hacia delante, echándose a un lado, para que no le vieran la cara. Milhombres avanzó, en dirección al entierro, pero su ayudante miró al abuelo de frente y se puso a gritar:

– ¡ES ÉL! ¡ES ÉL! ¡EL VAMPIRO VEJETE!

El abuelo dio media vuelta e iba a huir cuando
Madroño se lanzó hacia él y lo detuvo. Llegó un
policía, que andaba siempre por allí, y los separó.

—¡Este hombre es un vampiro! —gritó
Milhombres, a su vez, señalando al abuelo.

ESTÁN LOCOS.

ES EL VAMPIRO PERESTRELO.
MURIÓ HACE TRES AÑOS.

El policía, sin embargo, lo mantuvo a distancia.

—Lo que le decía. ¡Están locos!
Mire —dijo el abuelo
mostrando al policía
su carné de identidad.

—Gracias, señor
Meneses, no se moleste
—dijo el policía—. ¿Quiere
presentar una denuncia? Quizá intentaban robarle.

—No, no vale la pena —dijo el abuelo—. No me
han robado nada. Seguramente, solo ha sido una
confusión. A cualquiera puede pasarle.

—Aun así, me voy a llevar a estos dos pájaros
a la comisaría para identificarlos —dijo el policía.

SOY UN PROFESOR DE HISTORIA JUBILADO. UN CIUDADANO EJEMPLAR.

ESTO ES UN DISFRAZ. NO SOMOS ASÍ.

YA, YA. Y YO SOY EL PRÓXIMO REY DE INGLATERRA. VAMOS, DELANTE DE MÍ, QUE NO TENGO TODO EL DÍA.

CAPÍTULO VII
¡SURUCUPICU!

Milhombres y Madroño pasaron el resto del día en la comisaría de policía y no consiguieron salir hasta que ya había anochecido.

—Tan joven y ahora ya tengo **ANTEDECENTES** policiales. ¿Qué dirá mi mujer...?

—Cállese ya con su mujer. Y no se dice **«ANTEDECENTES»**, se dice **«ANTECEDENTES»**, que es incluirle en un registro, y esto no ha sido más que una identificación.

—¿Está seguro? Todavía soy muy joven. Y mi mujer me mata si no soy **CEDENTE**.

—**DECENTE**. Su mujer lo mata si no es **DECENTE**.

Madroño se detuvo, confuso.

—Entonces es **«ANTEDECENTES»**, ¿no?

Milhombres empujó al ayudante hacia delante, mientras decía:

—¿En qué fila estaba usted cuando repartieron la inteligencia?

Fueron a buscar las estacas de madera y después se dirigieron al cementerio.

TENEMOS QUE COMPROBAR QUE NO SE VA A DESPERTAR A UNA VIDA DE VAMPIRO. POR ESO, CUANDO EL ATAÚD SE AGITE O SE MUEVA, USTED VA Y ¡ZAS!, ESTACA EN EL CORAZÓN.

—Es la costumbre —dijo Madroño—. Pero estaba pensando en eso. Si matamos a una persona, es

UN CRIMEN

¿Si matamos a un vampiro, qué es?

Milhombres abrió los brazos para explicarse mejor:

—HOMBRE, MATAR A UN VAMPIRO ES UNA HONRA, UNA…

—¡NO DIGA ESO QUE VA A DECIR! —le advirtió Madroño.

—¿CÓMO SABE QUÉ IBA A DECIR? —preguntó Milhombres.

—Lo que iba a decir y digo ahora, hombre, es que matar a un vampiro es una honra una

Cuando dijo la palabra «felicidad» le cayó algo en la cabeza.

¡PLIM!

Era una especie de tornillo, todo chamuscado.

—¿De dónde ha salido eso? —preguntó Madroño mirando hacia arriba, y tuvo que hacerse a un lado para esquivar otro que caía a continuación.

Luego cayó una tuerca, también calcinada. Tuercas, tornillos... Todo aquello caía del cielo. Habían visto caer piedras pequeñas últimamente, casi por todas partes. Eran restos de otras mayores, que entraban en nuestra atmósfera (al parecer era la época) y se deshacían al pasar por ella. Los científicos lo habían explicado en la televisión. Pero ¿tornillos, tuercas y arandelas? No era de extrañar que Milhombres también perdiera un tornillo.

ALGUIEN ESTÁ HACIENDO ARREGLOS ALLÁ ARRIBA, EN EL CIELO. QUIZÁ SEA DIOS QUE INTENTA ARREGLAR EL MUNDO. PERO ESTO NO TIENE ARREGLO YA.

Milhombres no decía nada. Estaba conmocionado, confuso, desorientado.

—¿Está bien, profesor? —preguntó Madroño.

Y él nada. Quizá estaba viendo las estrellas sin mirar al cielo. Se notaba que en su cabeza también se formaban galaxias, constelaciones, agujeros negros. Todo lo que brillaba y giraba en el cielo estaba ahora en su cabeza. Por eso, no respondió.

Milhombres sonrió. Su sonrisa era abierta e inocente, la de alguien que está viendo las estrellas. Al fin, dijo muy alto:

¡SURUCUPICU!

AH, AHORA ESTÁ USTED **SURUCUPICU** DEBE SER PEOR QUE **SARAPITECO** PORQUE TIENE MUY MALA CARA.

Madroño llevó al profesor hasta la salida. Aquella operación también quedaba ahora comprometida.

Ya fuera, pasaron junto al policía que los había detenido.

—¿Otra vez por aquí? —les preguntó.

Y Milhombres dijo:

ES INCREÍBLE. TAN TEMPRANO Y YA VA BORRACHO. SI VUELVO A VERLOS POR AQUÍ...

Ellos apretaron el paso. Acababan de salir de la comisaría y no querían volver. La carrera le sentó bien a Milhombres, que se recuperó del efecto de la lluvia de tornillos y volvió en sí.

Se sentaron en un banco del jardín de la Rotonda de Buenavista, a la sombra de un árbol, para recuperarse del esfuerzo.

—Está visto que este no es nuestro día. Lo que me inquieta más es que he dicho Feli...

Estaba a mitad de la palabra cuando cayó una piedra hacia él que, por suerte, pudo esquivar en el último momento.

—¿Lo ve, Madroño? —dijo después—. Me ha salvado no decir la palabra completa; si no, la piedra me habría dado.

—Hace poco, cuando el profesor se volvió SURUCUPICU, eran tornillos.

YA SÉ LO QUE ES. AYER OÍ EN LA TELEVISIÓN QUE SON LOS RESTOS DEL CINTURÓN DE BASURA QUE RODEA EL PLANETA: CHATARRA DE SATÉLITES DESACTIVADOS, ETC.

LO QUE ME INQUIETA ES QUE CAYERON CUANDO DIJE UNA PALABRA CONCRETA... ¿QUÉ TENDRÁN CONTRA MÍ CIERTAS PALABRAS? SI AL MENOS FUERA CONTRA USTED, QUE LAS TRATA MAL...

—Calle, profesor. Es mejor estar callado —sugirió Madroño—. Es más seguro, ¿no?

Caminaron los dos, uno al lado
del otro, en silencio, siempre
mirando hacia arriba, no fuera
a caerles el cielo en la cabeza.

—Ay, ay, cuando me acuerdo
de que no voy a encontrar
en casa a mi padre...
—dijo Milhombres,
apesadumbrado—. Es tan
triste vivir solo.

En ese momento, Valentín,
cansado de andar, regresó a casa y se encerró en su

cuarto, después de
escapar de
Dientecilla,
que intentó
interesarlo de
nuevo en el
misterio del
almacén. «¡Ya
vale, ya vale!»,
le dijo. No quería
saber nada.

Todo lo llevaba por dentro. Incluso el hambre.
Poco tiempo después, esta le asaltó de veras y bajó
a la cocina en calcetines para que no lo oyeran.

Allí estaba Celeste acabando de arreglar la cocina.
Le dijo:

MAÑANA, VE A BUSCAR A ALEJO Y LLÉVALE
LOS CHORIZOS QUE VOY A DEJAR ENCIMA DE LA MESA
DE LA COCINA. ESTÁ EN LA PLAZA DE LAS FLORES.
ALEJO FLORISTA. ÉL TE AYUDARÁ
A ENCONTRAR A ESA MUCHACHA.

Valentín se animó. Encontrar a la muchacha era lo que más quería.

—Demasiadas preguntas —se quejó Celeste—. Solo puedo responder una. Así que escoge.

Él se puso a pensar.

—¿Solo una? —preguntó para ganar tiempo.

—Solo una —respondió ella—. Piénsatelo bien.

—¿Qué hora es? —quiso saber él.

—Son las once y media —respondió ella.

Después, se marchó.

—¡Eh! Aún no he hecho la pregunta —protestó Valentín.

—Perdona, pero acabo de responder una pregunta tuya —dijo ella—. Me has preguntado: «¿Qué hora es?»; y yo te he respondido: «Las once y media».

—Esa no era la pregunta que quería hacer —dijo Valentín.

ENTONCES NO DEBERÍAS
HABERLA HECHO.

Celeste se marchó, subiendo las escaleras.

Aun así, Valentín se animó por primera vez en todo ese día. Fuera quien fuese el florista, era una esperanza, una puerta que se abría. Puso un chorizo en un plato y se fue al salón, donde abrió la ventana grande de par en par, para sentir la brisa de la mañana.

Ah, era una brisa suave, perfumada, seguramente venía de lejos. ¿Del Mundo de Allá?

Índice